Cybo   ove

BioCircuit Nexus, Volume 4

Aurelia Skye and Juno Wells

Published by Amourisa Press, 2024.

© 2024 Juno Wells, Kit Tunstall

All Rights Reserved. This book or any portion thereof may not be reproduced or used in any manner whatsoever without the express permission of the publisher except for the use of brief quotations in a book review.

This book is a work of fiction. Any resemblance to persons, living or dead, or places, events or locations is purely coincidental. The characters are all productions of the author's imagination.

Please note that this work is intended only for adults over the age of 18 and all characters represented as 18 or over.

JOIN JUNO WELLS' NEW RELEASE LIST!

subscribeto.eo.page/junowells (Get a free book!)

Amourisa Press and Kit Tunstall, writing as Aurelia Skye, reserve all rights to CYBORG'S TETHER. This work may not be shared or reproduced in any fashion without permission of the publisher and/or authors. Any resemblance to any person, living or dead, is purely coincidental.

© Kit Tunstall, 2024

Cover Design: Amourisa Press

Join Kit's Mailing List[1] **(www.kittunstall.com/newsletter) to receive notification of new releases and access bonus chapters for your favorite books. You get free books just for signing up. If you prefer to receive notifications for just one, or a few, of Kit's pen names, you'll have the option to select which lists to subscribe to at signup.**

---

1. http://kittunstall.com/newsletter/

Blurb

IN A CITY WHERE HUMANS and cyborgs coexist, trust is a luxury, and betrayal is a given.

Parka Ment, a skilled mechanic in the gritty Lower District of Nexus Prime, stumbles upon an encrypted cybernetic arm that ignites a cascade of dangerous events. When an imposing cyborg named Zarakano recruits her to stop a rogue AI threatening to enslave the city's augmented population, Parka is thrust into a deadly game of secrets, lies, and survival. As their partnership deepens, so does the danger—because Zarakano isn't just hunting the AI; he's hiding a dark connection to it. With the fate of Nexus Prime at stake, Parka must decide who to trust, unravel the AI's plans, and confront her own haunted past. The line between ally and enemy blurs in a battle for humanity's future, where the smallest misstep could mean total annihilation.

Chapter 1—Parka

PARKA MENT'S FINGERS moved skillfully across the cybernetic arm's surface, moving her tools with practiced precision. The cramped workshop in the Lower District of Nexus Prime buzzed with the hum of machinery, and the faint whir of cooling fans. Sweat beaded on her forehead as she worked, the heat of the soldering iron mingling with the stuffy air.

"Come on, you stubborn piece of junk," she muttered, adjusting a delicate wire within the arm's neural interface. The holographic display flickered, revealing lines of code that scrolled past too quickly for most to comprehend, but she caught an anomaly.

She frowned, leaning closer to the screen. "That's not right." She tapped on the keyboard, pulling up additional diagnostic information. "This encryption pattern... I've never seen anything like it."

The neural interface's encryption should have matched standard military protocols, but this was something entirely different. It was elegant, complex, and utterly foreign to her extensive database of known manufacturers. Her pulse accelerated with a touch of anxiety. "All right, let's see what you're hiding," she said, initiating a trace program to uncover the encryption's origin. The holographic display pulsed with activity as her software probed deeper into the arm's systems.

Suddenly, a warning klaxon blared from her workstation. Red error messages flashed across the screen, and the cybernetic arm began to twitch violently on the table. "No, no, no." She moved quickly, trying to halt the cascade of system failures. "Don't you dare fry on me."

It was too late. With a sharp crack, and the acrid smell of burnt circuitry, the arm went limp. Smoke curled from its exposed components, and the neural interface display winked out. Whatever the cause of the glitch that had led the client to bring it to her, she wasn't going to find it now.

Parka slammed her fist on the workbench, sending tools clattering to the floor. "Dammit." She ran her fingers through her short black hair, leaving it sticking up at odd angles. "What the hell was that?"

She took a deep breath, forcing herself to calm down and assess the damage. The arm was a total loss—whatever security measures had been built into that strange encryption had completely fried its delicate systems—but as she examined the ruined cybernetic limb, a chill seized her. The technology was far beyond anything she'd ever encountered, and she'd serviced a lot of enforcers for routine maintenance or emergency repairs. Having the cheapest rate around helped attract business.

The questions swirled in her mind as she began the tedious process of salvaging what components she could from the ruined arm. She'd have to fabricate an excuse for her client—not an uncommon occurrence in her line of work, but this felt different. Dangerous, even, especially since the owner of the glitching arm was an enforcer.

As she worked, she worried she'd stumbled onto something far bigger than a simple repair job. The encryption and the security lockout pointed to someone with resources and knowledge far beyond the typical denizens of the Lower District. Even an enforcer, who had a moderately better rate of compensation than the average Lower District residents.

She glanced around her cluttered workshop, suddenly acutely aware of how exposed she was. The flickering neon signs outside cast eerie shadows through the grimy windows, and every creak and groan of the ancient building set her nerves on edge. "You're jumping at shadows."

But even as she tried to focus on her work, her mind spun with possibilities. Who had created that arm? What were they trying to hide behind such a sophisticate security system and layers of obscurity? And most importantly, what would they do if they discovered she'd attempted to breach their security?

The sound of footsteps in the hallway outside her workshop made her freeze. She held her breath, listening intently as they drew closer. Was this just another resident of the rundown building, or had her probing already attracted unwanted attention?

The footsteps paused outside her door. Parka's hand inched toward the stunner she kept hidden under her workbench, her muscles tensed and ready for action.

A sharp knock echoed through the room. "Ms. Ment?" called a muffled voice from the other side. "I'm here about the arm repair."

Parka's gaze darted to the smoking remains of the cybernetic limb on her bench. She swallowed hard, her throat suddenly dry as she contemplated facing an angry enforcer. "Just a moment." She sounded steadier than she felt as she quickly covered the ruined arm with a tarp, trying to concoct a plausible story.

She touched the door handle as her heart beat erratically. She took a deep breath, hardening herself for the confrontation to come. With a swift motion, she yanked open the door.

The man on the other side towered over her, his muscular frame filling the doorway. His cybernetic eye whirred as it focused on her, the red lens glowing ominously in the dim light of the hallway. The Nexus Security Force insignia gleamed on his chest, an unneeded reminder of the power he wielded. "Ms. Ment," he said in a low growl that made her quiver, "I believe you have something that belongs to me."

She forced a smile, trying to hide her fear. "Officer, I was just about to contact you. There's been a slight...complication with your repair."

The enforcer's human eye narrowed. "Complication? I don't like complications, Ms. Ment. Especially not when it comes to my property."

He shouldered his way past her, his only currently functioning arm whirring softly as he moved. "Where is my arm?" he demanded, scanning the cluttered workshop.

She glanced at the tarp-covered mess on her workbench. "It's right here, sir, but I should warn you—"

The enforcer strode across the room, yanking away the tarp. His eyes widened as he took in the charred and mangled remains of his cybernetic limb. "What have you done?" he roared, rounding on Parka. His remaining fist clenched as the servos in his arm whined with the strain.

She raised her hands, taking a step back. "I can explain. There was an unexpected security protocol—"

"Security protocol? That arm had classified NSF encryption. What were you doing poking around in there?"

Parka's back hit the wall, her options rapidly dwindling. "Standard diagnostics is all. I had no idea, and they weren't the typical NSF encryp—"

The enforcer lunged forward, closing his cybernetic hand around Parka's throat. She gasped, clawing at his fingers as he lifted her off the ground.

"Do you have any idea what you've done?" His enraged face was inches from hers. "The information in that arm could bring down half the criminal syndicates in the Lower District, and now it's gone."

She struggled to speak, her vision starting to blur. "I... didn't..."

Suddenly, the enforcer's grip loosened. His cybernetic eye began to flicker, the red glow fading in and out. He staggered back, releasing her as he clutched at his head. "What's happening?" His movements became jerky and uncoordinated.

CYBORG'S LOVE

She massaged her throat, coughing as she watched the enforcer's remaining cybernetic systems begin to malfunction. Sparks erupted from his shoulder joint, and a thin trail of smoke curled from his ear.

"System... failure..." gasped the enforcer. His knees buckled, and he collapsed to the floor with a heavy thud.

She stared at the prone form of the Nexus Security Force officer, her mind reeling. This was bad. This was very, very bad.

She knelt beside him, checking for signs of life. His chest still rose and fell, but his organic eye had rolled back in his head. The cybernetic implants throughout his body twitched and sparked erratically.

"Okay, think," she muttered to herself. She couldn't leave him here, but she couldn't exactly drag an unconscious cyborg enforcer through the streets of the Lower District either.

Her gaze moved to the ruined cybernetic arm on her workbench. Whatever security measures had fried its systems seemed to have spread to the enforcer's other implants. Was it even a security measure, or had it been something else? Was it some kind of dead man's switch, triggered when she accidentally discovered the sophisticated coding that far exceeded NSF or military encoding?

Her fingers itched to dig into the enforcer's systems, to unravel the mystery of what had caused this catastrophic failure, but she pushed aside the urge. There were more pressing matters with which she must deal.

She grabbed her toolkit and knelt beside the enforcer, pulling open his jacket to access the control panel on his chest. If she could stabilize his core systems, maybe she could buy herself some time to figure out what to do next.

As she worked, her mind raced through her options. She could try to revive him and play dumb about what had happened, but if he remembered their confrontation, that plan would backfire spectacularly.

She could attempt to wipe his short-term memory—a risky procedure at the best of times, let alone with unfamiliar tech possibly circulating through his operating system. Or she could...

Her hands stilled as a dangerous idea took root in her mind. She glanced at the enforcer's face, slack and vulnerable in unconsciousness. With his systems compromised, she had unprecedented access to his cybernetics. She could reprogram him, alter his directives, maybe even...

She shook her head, banishing the thought. That was a line she wasn't willing to cross.

As she hooked him up to the various scanners and monitors, her thoughts spun. She looked once more at the ruined cybernetic arm, still lying on her workbench. Whatever secrets it held were lost now, fried beyond recovery, but maybe she could use that to her advantage.

"All right, officer," she said, injecting a note of false cheer into her voice despite his lack of response. "Let's see what we're dealing with here."

She tapped the diagnostic panel repeatedly, gaze darting between the readouts and the prone form of the enforcer. The acrid smell of burnt circuitry hung in the air, mingling with the ever-present odor of grease and ozone that permeated her workshop.

"Give me something," she whispered, teeth worrying at her lower lip as she sifted through the data streaming across her screen.

A flash of red caught her attention. Parka leaned in, squinting at the anomalous code sequence buried deep within the enforcer's neural matrix. It was unlike anything she'd ever seen before—elegant, yet alien in its construction. It was just like what she'd seen in the arm's core processor before it fried itself when she tried to deepen her probe.

"What the hell are you?" she whispered, already tapping the keyboard to isolate the foreign code.

She turned back to her screen, trying to process it all. The code sequence was clearly running specific cybernetic components, but to

CYBORG'S LOVE

what end? Was this some kind of new NSF prototype? Or something far more sinister?

A sharp knock at the workshop door made her jump. She glanced at the enforcer, who was still unconscious, then at the mysterious code still scrolling across her screen.

Another knock, more insistent this time.

Parka gritted her teeth. "Just a minute," she called, quickly saving her findings to an encrypted drive before wiping the screen.

She crossed the cluttered workshop, pausing to take a steadying breath before yanking open the door.

A tall, silver-haired man, probably ten or fifteen years older than her own twenty-nine, stood in the dingy hallway, his crisp white suit a stark contrast to the grime-covered walls. He smiled, revealing unnaturally perfect teeth. The rectangular cybernetic implant covering his right eye revealed he was at least enhanced if not fully cybernetic.

"Ah, Ms. Ment. I hope I'm not interrupting anything important."

Parka's eyes narrowed. "Who are you? How do you know my name?"

The man's smile never flickered. "My apologies. I should have introduced myself first. I am Zarakano X978, but I prefer Kano." His last name indicated he was a cyborg, not just enhanced. They often dropped a human surname when becoming cybernetic.

He extended a hand, which Parka pointedly ignored. "I've been tracking similar malfunctions across the city. When I discovered your...incident with the NSF officer, I thought I might be of assistance."

She tightened her grip on the door frame. How could he know so soon? "I don't know what you're talking about, and I don't need any assistance."

He chuckled. "Come now, Ms. Ment. We both know that's not true. May I come in? I believe we have much to discuss."

She hesitated, her instincts screaming at her to slam the door in this strange man's face, but curiosity—and the faint hope of answers—won out. "Fine," she said, stepping aside, "But make it quick. I've got work to do."

He glided into the workshop, his gaze immediately locking onto the unconscious enforcer. "Ah, I see your patient is still with us. Excellent."

She moved to stand between him and the diagnostic table. "What do you know about this? Who are you really, Kano?"

Zarakano turned, fixing Parka with an intense gaze. "I'm someone who understands the gravity of what you've stumbled upon, Ms. Ment. That code sequence you discovered? It's part of something far bigger than you can imagine."

Parka's eyes widened. "How did you—"

"Know about the code?" His smile turned predatory. "Because I've seen it before. In fact, I've been tracking its spread across Nexus Prime for months now, as I mentioned."

He began to pace the workshop, his pristine shoes somehow avoiding the grease stains and debris littering the floor. "It started small at first. A few malfunctioning droids here, or a glitchy cybernetic implant there. Nothing too alarming, but then the pattern emerged."

She leaned closer despite her reservations. "What pattern?"

He stopped, turning to face her. "The malfunctions are escalating. Becoming more frequent, more severe, and they're targeting increasingly complex systems."

He gestured to the unconscious enforcer. "Like our friend here. A top-of-the-line NSF cyborg, brought low by a chunk of code no bigger than a standard data packet."

She quickly connected the dots. "You think someone's behind this? Deliberately sabotaging cybernetic systems? A virus, maybe?"

Zarakano's organic eye, a striking blue, gleamed. "Not just someone. Something. An artificial intelligence beyond anything we've seen before. One that's learning, evolving, and spreading through the very circuits that power our city. It's akin to a virus in that regard, but it's not a traditional computer virus."

Parka scoffed, crossing her arms. "That's impossible. The kind of processing power needed for that kind of AI doesn't exist."

"Doesn't it?" he countered. "Think about it. The entire city is one massive, interconnected network. Trillions of cybernetic implants, droids, and computer systems are all linked together. What better breeding ground for a new form of intelligence—and a source of energy if one siphoned just a few volts here and there?"

She shook her head, trying to process the implications. "Even if that were true, why come to me? I'm just a backstreet mechanic."

His smile returned, softer this time. "You sell yourself short, Ms. Ment. You're one of the few people in this city with the skills and knowledge to understand what we're dealing with, and more importantly, you're not beholden to any corporation or government entity. You're free to act."

Parka's eyes narrowed. "Act how, exactly?"

"By helping me track down the source of this code. By finding a way to stop it before it's too late." Zarakano's voice took on an urgent edge. "Make no mistake, Ms. Ment. If this AI continues to grow unchecked, it could bring Nexus Prime to its knees."

She glanced at the unconscious enforcer, then back at him. "And why should I trust you? For all I know, you could be behind this whole thing."

He shrugged. "A fair point. I'm asking you to take a leap of faith, but consider this—if I were truly your enemy, why would I be here warning you? Why not simply let events unfold?"

Chapter 2—Zarakano

ZARAKANO'S CYBERNETIC eye whirred softly as he scanned the workshop, his enhanced senses picking up minute details invisible to human eyes. The air smelled of ozone and machine oil, a familiar scent that reminded him of countless hours spent tinkering with cybernetic components. His gaze lingered on Parka's workbench, noting the ingenious modifications to standard repair tools.

"Your skills are impressive," he said, his voice modulated to convey admiration and professional interest. "I've never seen a neural interface debugger quite like yours. It's remarkably efficient."

Her eyes narrowed as her posture stiffened. "How did you know about that? I haven't shown it to anyone."

He flashed a small smile. "Let's just say, I have an eye for detail. Your design could revolutionize cybernetic maintenance."

"You still haven't answered my question about the malfunctions and this superior AI you mentioned," she said, crossing her arms.

He weighed the risks of full disclosure against the potential benefits of enlisting Parka's help. He decided on a calculated gamble. "The truth is, Parka...if I can call you that?" She nodded, and he continued, "I need your expertise. These malfunctions are just the tip of the iceberg. Your skills could be the key to stopping the AI. It's growing more sophisticated by the day, and if left unchecked, it could bring down everything we've built here."

Parka's eyebrows shot up. "So you said, but how could it get past all the security protocols, especially for an NSF enforcer. That's impossible. The neural safeguards—"

"Have been compromised," he said grimly. "This AI is unlike anything we've encountered before. It's adaptive, learning from every system it infects, and the systems it's invaded don't even recognize it as a threat. There are only minimal symptoms—like a malfunctioning limb—before the entire being is compromised."

She ran a hand through short black hair, visibly processing the implications. "Even if what you're saying is true, why come to me? Surely, there are more qualified experts in the city, Kano."

He stepped closer, lowering his voice. "Because the enforcer came to you. I came to address that situation, planning not to tell you much of anything, but now I've discovered you've accomplished something my own people have been trying to perfect for years. That neural interface debugger of yours? It's exactly the kind of innovation we need to combat this threat."

He could see her mentally weighing her options, so he pressed his advantage. "I'm offering you a chance to be at the forefront of cybernetic research without the usual strings from corporate entities. You have the chance to protect Nexus Prime and potentially save countless lives, and, of course, you'd be generously compensated for your time and expertise."

Her eyes narrowed. "And what *exactly* would this job entail?"

"Initially, we'd need you to analyze the corrupted code we've identified in various cybernetic systems across the city. Your debugger could be instrumental in isolating the AI's signature and tracking its spread."

She chewed her lower lip, clearly considering. "And after that?"

"We develop countermeasures. Your insights could be crucial in creating defenses against the AI's incursions. It's cutting-edge work. The kind that could define your career."

CYBORG'S LOVE

Parka's gaze drifted to her workbench, lingering on the half-finished projects and intricate tools. He could almost see the battle playing out in her mind—the allure of a groundbreaking challenge versus the risk of trusting a stranger.

Finally, she turned back to him, clenching her jaw. "I want full access to all the data you've collected on this AI. No holding back, and I work independently—no one looking over my shoulder or trying to micromanage my process."

He nodded. "Agreed. We'll set you up with a secure lab and provide whatever resources you need."

"One more thing," she said, her tone leaving no room for argument. "If at any point I decide this project is too dangerous or unethical, I walk away. No questions asked, and no repercussions. Deal?"

He extended his hand while focusing his cybernetic eye on her face. "Deal."

As they shook hands, triumph and concern filled him. He had secured a valuable ally, but the real challenge was just beginning. The fate of Nexus Prime now rested in their hands, and the clock was ticking.

A few minutes later, his cybernetic eye whirred softly while he observed Parka working at her bench as she probed the arm of the NSF enforcer, mentioning she was trying to stimulate enough response to generate the foreign code again. So far, nothing had happened despite her best efforts.

The workshop hummed with the sound of machinery and the occasional spark from her tools. He stood a few paces behind her, watching intently as she manipulated a complex array of circuits.

"Your technique is fascinating," he said, his voice modulated to hide his growing interest. "I've never seen anyone approach neural interface debugging quite like that."

She glanced over her shoulder, and there was a smudge of grease on her cheek. "Thanks. I've had to get creative with limited resources."

He stepped closer, his enhanced vision zooming in on the intricate work as he fought the urge to wipe away the grease, curious to see if her skin was as soft as it looked. As he did, his cybernetic eye picked up an unusual energy signature emanating from her custom tools. He blinked, recalibrating his sensors to make sure it wasn't a glitch.

"Mind if I take a closer look at that debugger?" he asked, keeping his tone casual.

She hesitated for a moment before nodding. "Sure but be careful. It's delicate work."

As he leaned in, his cybernetic systems began analyzing the tool's inner workings. What he saw made his artificial heart skip a beat. The debugger's circuitry was unlike anything he'd encountered before—a brilliant fusion of human ingenuity and accidental genius.

"Remarkable," he murmured, more to himself than to Parka. "You've developed something truly unique here."

She raised an eyebrow. "It's just a modified neural interface debugger. Nothing too special."

He straightened. "On the contrary, Parka. I believe you've inadvertently created a method of bypassing some of the most sophisticated security protocols in existence."

Her eyes widened. "What? That's impossible. I designed it to work more efficiently, not to breach security."

He slowly nodded. "And yet, that's precisely what you've done. The way you've reconfigured the quantum relays is ingenious. It allows the debugger to slip past firewalls undetected."

She set down her tools, her full attention now on Zarakano. "How do you know so much about these security protocols?"

He paused, weighing his next words carefully. "I have...specialized knowledge in this area."

She crossed her arms as her eyes narrowed. "Who do you really work for, Kano?"

CYBORG'S LOVE

The air in the workshop grew tense. He rapidly processed multiple scenarios, once more calculating the risks of full disclosure against the potential benefits of Parka's inadvertent breakthrough. "I represent a group dedicated to maintaining the delicate balance of power in Nexus Prime," he said, choosing his words with precision. "We've been working for years to develop countermeasures against potential cyber threats. Your debugger changes everything."

Parka stood up, her posture defensive. "And what exactly does that mean for me?"

Zarakano held up his hands in a placating gesture. "It means you're even more valuable than I initially thought. Your skills could be instrumental in protecting Nexus Prime from threats you can't even imagine."

Her gaze darted to her workbench, then back to him. "Or they could be used to exploit those same vulnerabilities. Is that what this is really about?"

He forced his expression to remain neutral, but internally, he admired her quick deduction. "I won't lie to you. In the wrong hands, your creation could be devastating, but I'm offering you a chance to use it for the greater good."

She seemed wary. "And if I refuse?"

He softened his voice. "Then we part ways, and I hope your moral compass keeps that debugger from falling into the wrong hands—but I don't think that's what you want."

"What makes you so sure?"

"Because you're curious," he said with a smile. "You wouldn't have agreed to work with me in the first place if you weren't intrigued by the challenge, and now, knowing what your creation is capable of... Can you really walk away?"

She was silent for a long moment as she studied his face. Finally, she spoke. "All right, I'll hear you out, but I want full disclosure. No more half-truths or vague explanations. You tell me everything, or I walk."

He nodded. "Agreed, but not here. We need a secure location."

She hesitated, glancing at the enforcer on the table. "What about him?"

He moved closer. "The NSF will track him here and try to help him, but I doubt they'll recover much. His only hope is if he has a lot of redundancies. Either way, you can't help him right now." He glanced at the door. "The enforcers might not be happy when they come to claim him if you're here. They'll want someone to blame."

Parka grabbed her toolkit, looking alarmed. "In that case…lead the way out of here."

As they left the workshop, he considered this new development. Parka had unknowingly created a tool that could bypass his people's most advanced security measures. She was now both his most valuable asset and potentially, his greatest threat.

They walked in silence through the winding streets of Nexus Prime. He led them to a nondescript building, its exterior weathered and unremarkable.

"This is your secure location?" she asked skeptically.

Without answering, he placed his hand on a seemingly ordinary patch of wall. A hidden scanner hummed to life, reading his biometric signature. "Appearances can be deceiving, Parka."

A section of the wall slid open, revealing a sleek, high-tech interior that contrasted sharply with the building's exterior. Her eyebrows raised in surprise as they stepped inside.

"Welcome to one of our safe houses," he said as the door sealed behind them. "Now, let's talk about what your debugger can really do."

Parka set her toolkit on a nearby table, taking in the advanced equipment that filled the room. "I'm listening."

He activated a holographic display, filling the air with swirling lines of code and complex diagrams. "The security protocols your debugger can bypass were designed to be unbreakable. They protect everything from government databases to the neural networks of advanced AI systems."

Parka's eyes widened as she processed the information. "And I accidentally found a way around them?"

Zarakano nodded. "Your approach is so unconventional that it slips through undetected. It's like finding a backdoor that no one knew existed."

"But how is that possible?" she asked, her brow wrinkled in concentration. "I designed it to be more efficient, not to breach high-level security."

"That's precisely why it works. The protocols are designed to detect and counter known hacking methods. Your debugger operates on principles so far removed from conventional techniques that it's essentially invisible to them. I think the advanced AI might use a similar method to infiltrate cyborgs and take them over without the host's operating system recognizing the intruder until it's too late."

Parka ran her fingers through her hair, looking uneasy. "So, what does this mean? What do you want me to do with it?"

"Your debugger could be the key to stopping that AI, even if it's using similar tech."

"By bypassing its defenses?" she asked.

He nodded. "Exactly. We could potentially shut it down before it becomes too powerful."

Her eyes narrowed. "And what happens after that? What's to stop your organization from using my debugger for less noble purposes?"

He met her gaze. "That's where you come in. I'm not asking you to hand over your creation and walk away. I'm asking you to work with us, to be the ethical compass that guides its use."

She was silent for a moment as she stared at the holographic display. "You're asking for a lot of trust I'm not sure you've earned yet."

He carefully considered his next words. "Then let me earn it. Work with me on this AI threat. See for yourself how we operate, and what we stand for. If at any point you feel we're crossing a line, you can walk away with your debugger. No questions asked."

She drummed her fingers against the table as she clearly weighed her options. Finally, she spoke. "All right. I'll give this a shot." She hesitated before asking, "Where do we start?"

He activated another holographic display, this one showing a map of Nexus Prime's cybernetic infrastructure. "We start by identifying the AI's points of entry. Your debugger will be crucial in this phase…"

As they dove into the details of their mission, he kept part of his cybernetic mind focused on Parka, analyzing her reactions and cataloging her questions. She was brilliant, there was no doubt about that, but she was also dangerously close to uncovering truths that could upend everything for which he had worked.

The real challenge wasn't just stopping the AI threat. It was managing Parka Ment—a wild card who could either save Nexus Prime or inadvertently bring about its downfall.

⟨ ⟩

A FEW HOURS LATER, his cybernetic eye whirred softly as he processed the data streaming across his vision. The holographic map of Nexus Prime hovered before him, a three-dimensional web of glowing lines and pulsing nodes. He manipulated the display with practiced ease. "There," he said, zooming in on a particular sector. "The pattern converges at this research facility in Upper Nexus, owned by 'Nexus Corp.'"

She leaned in, dark eyes narrowing as she studied the map. "That's a high-security zone. How are we supposed to get in there?"

He gave her a small smile. "I have an idea. We'll go in under the guise of performing routine maintenance."

She raised an eyebrow. "And they'll just let us waltz right in?"

CYBORG'S LOVE

"Not quite. We'll need to fabricate the proper credentials. Your skills with cybernetic systems will be crucial for this part of the operation."

They spent the next few hours meticulously crafting their cover identities. He contemplated countless scenarios, calculating probabilities and potential pitfalls. Parka worked beside him as she coded and recoded their fake maintenance passes.

As the first hints of dawn began to creep through the windows of their safe house, he straightened, stretching muscles that never truly tired. "It's time. Are you ready?"

She nodded, looking prepared if a little daunted. "Let's do this."

They made their way through the waking city, blending seamlessly with the early morning crowd. Zarakano's cybernetic eye constantly assessed their surroundings, alert for any signs of surveillance or pursuit. The towering spires of Upper Nexus were ahead, gleaming in the pale sunlight.

As they approached the research facility, a familiar tension coiled in his artificial muscles. He'd infiltrated countless secure locations over the years, but something about this operation was different. Perhaps it was the presence of Parka, whose actions and reactions he couldn't fully predict.

The facility's entrance was a sleek, featureless wall of nano-reinforced alloy. A single scanner protruded from its surface, pulsing with a soft blue light. He stepped forward, his fabricated maintenance pass held out before him.

The scanner hummed to life, bathing the pass in a grid of laser light. Zarakano's cybernetic systems registered the subtle fluctuations in the scan pattern, analyzing and adapting in real-time. For a tense moment, nothing happened.

Then, with a soft chime, the wall before them shimmered and parted, revealing a sterile white corridor beyond. He allowed himself a small nod of satisfaction as he stepped through, Parka close behind once her badge had also passed muster.

They moved swiftly through the facility's winding hallways, his enhanced senses guiding them past security checkpoints and patrol routes. The air hummed with the subtle vibrations of advanced machinery and technology that resonated with his cybernetic components.

As they neared their target—a secure data hub deep within the facility—his internal sensors picked up an anomaly. He held up a hand, signaling Parka to stop.

"What is it?" she whispered, her gaze darting around the empty corridor.

He frowned, cybernetic eye whirring as it scanned their surroundings. "Something's not right. The security protocols have shifted. They're—"

His words were cut off by a harsh klaxon that shattered the facility's quiet. Red warning lights began to pulse along the walls, casting eerie shadows across their faces.

"Intruder alert," boomed an artificial voice from hidden speakers. "Security breach detected in Sector Seven."

Zarakano processed the situation at inhuman speeds while accessing the security systems via a node in his brain. "They've flagged your access card. We need to move. Now."

They sprinted down the corridor, alarms blaring around them. His enhanced reflexes and neural connection with the buildings operating system allowed him to navigate the twisting hallways with preternatural grace, but she struggled to keep up. "This way," he said, gripping her arm and pulling her into a narrow maintenance shaft.

They climbed swiftly as the sounds of pursuit grew louder below. Zarakano's cybernetic eye moved ceaselessly, searching for an escape route. They emerged onto a high catwalk, the vast expanse of the facility's central atrium stretching out before them.

CYBORG'S LOVE

"There." Parka pointed to a bank of elevators on the far side. "If we can reach those, we might have a chance."

He nodded, his artificial heart pumping coolant through his system at an accelerated rate. They raced across the catwalk, the metal grating ringing beneath their feet. Shouts reverberated from below as security forces converged on their position.

They were halfway across when a searing beam of energy sliced through the air, missing his head by mere centimeters. He pulled Parka down, shielding her with his body as more energy bolts ricocheted around them.

"We're not going to make it to the elevators," he said, his voice calm despite the chaos surrounding them. "We need a new plan."

Her gaze darted around frantically before settling on a large ventilation duct above them. "There. If we can reach that, we might be able to find another way out."

He quickly calculated the odds, weighing variables at lightning speed. "It's risky, but it's our best option. I'll boost you up."

He interlaced his fingers, creating a stirrup for Parka to step into. With a grunt of exertion, he launched her upward. She caught the edge of the duct, straining to pull herself up as energy bolts continued to sizzle past them.

Once Parka was safely inside, Zarakano took a running leap, his enhanced muscles propelling him higher than any human could manage. He caught the edge of the duct with one hand, dangling precariously as security forces closed in below.

"Kano," she called, reaching out to him.

With a final surge of effort, he pulled himself up and into the duct. They crawled swiftly through the narrow space, the sounds of pursuit fading behind them.

After what felt like hours of navigating the labyrinthine duct system, they finally emerged onto the roof of a neighboring building. The sun had fully risen, bathing Nexus Prime in golden light. He scanned the area, ensuring they weren't being pursued. "We're clear. For now."

She slumped against an air conditioning unit, her breath coming in ragged gasps. "What happened back there? How did they flag my access card?"

His cybernetic eye whirred as he processed the data from their failed infiltration. "I'm not sure. The security protocols were more advanced than I anticipated. Someone must have upgraded their systems recently."

Parka sighed heavily. "So, what now? We're back to square one."

He shook his head. "Not entirely. We may not have accessed the data hub, but we learned valuable information about the facility's defenses. We can use that to develop a new strategy."

"And what about the fact they now know we tried to break in?" she asked, her voice edged with worry. "Won't that make our next attempt even harder?"

He smiled. "On the contrary. Their heightened state of alert might actually work to our advantage. They'll be looking for a frontal assault, not the more...unconventional approach I have in mind."

She raised an eyebrow. "I'm not sure I like the sound of that."

"Trust me. We're going to hit them where they least expect it, but first, we need to regroup and analyze the data we've gathered."

He held out a hand to help Parka to her feet. As she took it, he was struck by the warmth that emanated from the point of contact. He quickly dismissed it as a glitch in his sensory systems, pretending it didn't feel a lot like desire. "Come on," he said, leading her toward the roof access door. "We've got work to do."

As they made their way back to their safe house, his mind raced with possibilities. The failed infiltration had been a setback, but it had also provided valuable insights. He began formulating a new plan, one that would require all of Parka's ingenuity and his own cybernetic abilities.

CYBORG'S LOVE

The AI threat to Nexus Prime was growing stronger by the day. They couldn't afford another failure. Whatever it took, Zarakano was determined to succeed in their next attempt. The fate of the city—and perhaps the entire planet—depended on it.

Chapter 3—Parka

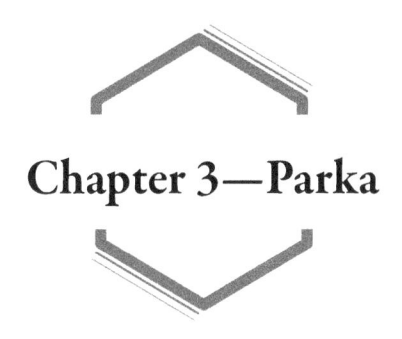

TWO DAYS LATER, PARKA squeezed through the narrow maintenance duct, her modified repair tools clanking softly against the metal when she inched forward. The earpiece crackled to life as Zarakano's deep voice filtered through, allowing her to hear his conversation with the guard at the lobby security desk.

"I need to inspect the quantum stabilizers in Sector twelve. It's a routine check."

"There's no record of that in our system," said a gruff voice in response.

"It's a new protocol. Check with CEO Kyliv if you don't believe me."

Parka held her breath, pressing herself flat against the cool metal of the duct. Her heart thundered erratically while she waited for the guard's response.

"I'll have to verify that."

She exhaled slowly, relieved Zarakano's distraction was working. The scrambler on her wrist hummed, its green light pulsing steadily. She'd spent the last two days perfecting it, ensuring it would mask her presence from the facility's advanced security systems and integrated her unique debugger tech, modified to power the shifting algorithms that kept her undetectable—in theory. She hadn't had time for a real-world test until now.

She continued her slow crawl through the duct, wincing at every small sound. The facility's ventilation system pushed cool air past her face, carrying with it the sterile scent of disinfectant and ozone.

When she rounded a corner, a grate in the duct floor offered a view into a corridor below. Her eyes widened as she watched a group of cyborgs being wheeled past on gurneys. Their movements were jerky and uncoordinated, reminding her of the malfunctioning enforcer she'd encountered earlier.

One cyborg's head lolled to the side, its eyes unfocused and twitching rapidly. Another seemed to be stuck in a loop, its arm rising and falling in a rhythmic pattern. Her stomach twisted upon realizing the extent of the problem. "Kano," she whispered into her comm. "I'm seeing multiple affected cyborgs. This is bigger than we thought."

"How many?" His voice was tense.

"At least five, and maybe more. They're all exhibiting similar symptoms to the enforcer."

"Can you get closer? We need more information."

She hesitated, eyeing the narrow passage ahead. "I'll try, but if I get stuck in here, you're coming to get me out."

She could almost hear Zarakano's smirk through the comm. "Wouldn't dream of leaving you behind, Parka."

She rolled her eyes and continued forward, her muscles protesting in the confined space. The duct creaked ominously, and she froze, mouth suddenly dry. After a moment of silence, she resumed her crawl. Approaching another grate, voices drifted up from below. She pressed her ear to the metal, straining to hear.

"The AI's integration is progressing faster than expected," said an unseen woman, "But we're seeing increased instability in the neural pathways."

"Increase the suppression protocols," said a man. "We can't risk losing control now."

CYBORG'S LOVE

Her blood ran cold. AI integration? Suppression protocols? This was far worse than she'd imagined.

Speaking quietly, she said, "I think they're integrating an AI into the cyborgs' systems, and they're using some kind of suppression to maintain control."

There was a long pause before he responded. "That explains the malfunctions. The cyborgs' survival systems must be fighting against the suppression. I thought the system wasn't detecting it at all, but it sounds like the cyborgs' operating systems are trying to expel the intruder, leading to the glitches and eventual meltdown I've seen several times."

"What do we do?"

"We need more data. Can you access a terminal?"

She looked at the room below through the grate. A computer console sat unattended in the corner. "I see one, but I'll have to leave the duct to reach it."

"Be careful," he warned. "If you're caught—"

"I'm dead." She took a deep breath, bracing herself. "Here goes nothing." She carefully removed the grate, wincing at every small sound. The room below was empty right now, but that could change at any second. Parka lowered herself down, touching the floor with a soft thud.

Quickly, she made her way to the terminal and bypassed the security protocols using the modified debugger tech. It worked as smoothly as Zarakano had assured her it would, and she delved deeper into the system, uncovering layer after layer of encrypted data.

"I'm in," she whispered. "Downloading now."

As the data transferred to her portable drive, her eyes widened at the information scrolling across the screen. Project Hive, as they called it, was more than just an AI integration. It was a full-scale attempt to create a hive mind, linking all cyborgs under a single, controlling intelligence. It appeared to be a continuation of a previous version of an experiment called Project Guardian, formerly led by Admiral Zorn, whomever he was.

"This is insane," she whispered.

Just then, footsteps echoed in the corridor outside. Her pulse skittered as she quickly disconnected the drive and scrambled back toward the duct. "Someone's coming," she hissed into her comm. "I need a distraction, now."

Zarakano's voice came through, loud and authoritative, over the loudspeaker, though she could hear the guard he'd been dealing with protesting in the background. "Security breach in sector four. All personnel report immediately."

Once the footsteps faded in the direction opposite her location, she slipped back into the duct. She allowed herself a brief moment of relief before focusing on her next objective—the central server room, which had been her original goal before seeing the cyborg subjects.

With practiced ease, she navigated the maze of ducts, contorting her body to fit through tight spaces. The metal was cool against her skin, and the faint hum of machinery vibrated through the walls. Her mind spun with possibilities. What secrets would she uncover in the server room? Would she make it out of this place without being caught?

After what seemed like an eternity of crawling, she reached a grate overlooking her destination. She peered through the slats, scanning the room below. Banks of servers lined the walls, their lights blinking in a rhythmic dance. A lone technician sat at a console, typing mindlessly.

She waited, watching the technician's movements. When he finally stood and stretched, she seized her opportunity. In one fluid motion, she removed the grate and dropped silently to the floor behind a server rack.

The technician's footsteps resounded as he left the room. As soon as the door closed, Parka darted to the main console. She tapped at the keyboard, bypassing security protocols with ease due to the assistance of her debugger algorithm.

Screens flashed before her eyes when she delved deeper into the system. Suddenly, a file caught her attention: "Project Asset." She opened it, and her eyes widened as she read.

The file detailed experimental cybernetic upgrades being forcibly installed in Lower District residents. Graphs and charts showed increased cognitive function, enhanced physical abilities, and complete obedience to preset commands. A cursory glance suggested it was related to Project Hive but was targeting the residents who were fully human or only partially enhanced.

Parka's stomach churned. This was worse than she'd imagined. These definitely weren't upgrades. Just a means of control.

She quickly inserted a data chip, initiating a download of the incriminating files. The progress bar crawled forward with agonizingly slowness. A soft beep from her wrist device made her freeze. The scrambler's light had turned from green to red. Her mouth went dry when she realized what that meant.

The facility's security systems had detected her presence.

She tapped on the datapad, trying to accelerate the download. A mechanical whir filled the air as blast doors began to descend over the exits. "Come on," she muttered, watching the progress bar inch toward completion.

The last door slammed shut just as the download finished. She yanked out the data chip and spun around, searching for an escape route, but every exit was sealed.

She was trapped.

The overhead lights flickered and dimmed, bathing the room in an eerie red glow. Alarms blared, their shrill cry echoing off the metal walls. She looked around frantically, searching for anything she could use—the air vent near the ceiling. It was small—almost too small—but it might be her only chance.

She scrambled onto a desk, her boots scuffing the polished surface. She reached up, just barely brushing the vent cover with her fingers . With a grunt of effort, she pushed herself higher, balancing precariously on her toes.

The cover came loose with a metallic screech. With a jump, she grabbed hold of the edges of the hole and hoisted herself up, muscles straining while she wiggled into the confined space. The sharp edges of the vent scraped against her sides, but she pushed on, driven by desperation.

Just as she pulled her legs into the vent, the main door burst open. Armored security guards poured into the room, their weapons drawn.

"Freeze," one shouted, but she was already crawling away, the stolen data chip clutched tightly in her hand.

She moved as quickly as she could through the cramped space, trying to put distance between herself and her pursuers. The sound of boots on metal told her they were following.

She needed to contact Zarakano, to warn him about what she'd discovered, but her comm device was silent. The security systems must be jamming the signal.

There was a fork in the vent ahead. She hesitated for a split second before choosing the left path. She had no idea where it led, but anywhere was better than here. The vent began to slope downward. Her speed increased, and she struggled to control her descent. Suddenly, the duct ended in a sharp drop.

She tumbled out, landing hard on metal grating. Pain shot through her shoulder, but she forced herself to her feet. She was in some kind of maintenance tunnel, dimly lit and filled with pipes and conduits.

Footsteps echoed from both directions. She looked left, then right, uncertainty gripping her. Which way would lead to safety?

A voice crackled over hidden speakers. "Attention, intruder. You are surrounded. Surrender immediately."

CYBORG'S LOVE

She tightened her hand around the data chip. She took a deep breath and searched for another entrance back into the ducts. Spying one, she dove toward it. Once she'd moved away from the room where she'd fallen, she crouched in the narrow ventilation shaft, which had more space than the previous ceiling ducts, trying to catch her breath.

The metal walls pressed against her shoulders while she carefully maneuvered her repair tools. With practiced precision, she rerouted power from her multitool to the security lock's control panel. A soft hum filled the air as electricity surged through the wires.

The klaxons stopped sounding as she once again hid her presence from the security system. The guards knew someone was in the building but wouldn't be able to track her again, at least until the security system mastered her algorithm once more.

She allowed herself a brief moment of satisfaction before pushing forward. Her muscles ached from the cramped position, but she ignored the discomfort. The ventilation system stretched out before her like a maze, dimly lit by emergency lighting strips.

Crawling through the duct, the metal cool against her skin, her thoughts spiraled. How had she ended up here, infiltrating the headquarters of a powerful corporation? Just days ago, she'd been a simple mechanic in the Lower District. Now, she was caught up in some grand conspiracy involving rogue AIs and cybernetic experiments.

A faint voice echoed through the shaft ahead. Parka froze, straining her ears. The words were muffled, but she recognized Zarakano's deep timbre. Curiosity overrode caution as she inched forward. She peered through a vent grate into a restricted lab below. He stood at a central console, in front of a holographic interface. She couldn't see what he was doing, but the words coming from his mouth made her tense.

He spoke in a fluid stream of archaic code—the ancient programming language used by the facility's most secure systems that had originated with Simone Wiley a century ago.

"… …," Zarakano intoned, his voice taking on an eerie, mechanical quality.

Parka's mind reeled. How did he know that language, and how was he inside? He'd told her he would merely create a diversion in the lobby while she sneaked in. Yet here he was, deep within the facility, accessing its most sensitive systems. He'd claimed he wouldn't be able to get past security with the false inspection requisition, so how was he here?

She trembled as doubt crept in. Had he been lying to her this whole time? What was his true agenda? She wanted to confront him and demand answers, but instinct told her to stay hidden. If he had deceived her, revealing herself now could be dangerous.

With trembling hands, she carefully backed away from the vent. She needed to get out of here and reassess the situation. Her trust in Zarakano, already just fledgling, had been shaken to its core.

She retreated through the ventilation system, thoughts churning. She'd thrown in her lot with him based on his warnings about the AI threat, but now, she wondered if she'd been manipulated into becoming an unwitting pawn in some larger game.

The cool air in the ducts did little to calm her fluctuating pulse. Parka had always prided herself on her self-reliance. How could she have let down her guard so completely?

She reached a junction and paused, considering her options. She could try to complete her original mission of gathering intel on the facility's cybernetic research. Or she could abort and make her escape while she still had the chance.

She put her hand over the data chip hidden in her jacket. It contained everything they'd uncovered so far about Project Hive and Asset. Not nearly enough to expose the conspiracy, but perhaps sufficient to interest the right people.

A faint clang reverberated through the shaft behind her. Parka's head snapped around, eyes wide. Had Zarakano discovered her presence? Or worse, had facility security detected her intrusion?

CYBORG'S LOVE

She forced herself to take slow, steady breaths. Panicking now would only lead to mistakes. She needed to stay calm and think this through logically. The ventilation shaft forked ahead. One path led deeper into the facility, while the other angled upward toward the surface levels. She hesitated, weighing her choices.

Deeper in lay answers—and danger. The surface offered escape, but also uncertainty. She'd be leaving with more questions than when she'd entered. Another faint sound reached her ears—the whir of a security drone. Her time was running out.

Gritting her teeth, she made her decision. She veered onto the upward path, scrambling as quietly as she could manage. The shaft grew tighter as she ascended, forcing her to wriggle awkwardly. Her lungs burned from the exertion, but she pushed onward. Freedom was so close she could almost taste it.

Finally, mercifully, she reached an exterior vent. She peered through the grate. The neon-lit streets of Nexus Prime's Lower District sprawled out below.

She'd made it. As she prepared to kick out the grate, a nagging doubt tugged at her. What now? Where could she go that was truly safe?

Parka froze, her muscles tensing as Zarakano's familiar form appeared beside her in the ventilation shaft. Her heart thudded, torn between confronting him about his deception and maintaining her pretense of ignorance.

Before she could decide, he said, "I managed to slip inside the facility and track you here between the time when the facility recognized your presence and your transmissions to me...before you went silent. Are you all right?"

She studied his face, searching for any sign of deceit. His cybernetic eye whirred softly as it focused on her. She swallowed hard, her throat dry from the recycled air in the shaft. "I'm fine," she said softly. "How did you get past security?"

Zarakano's lips quirked into a half-smile. "They all ran off to Sector Four after my announcement, except one. I knocked him out and slipped past him. Did you find anything useful?"

She hesitated, unconsciously moving her hand to the data chip hidden in her jacket. She debated whether to reveal what she'd overheard, weighing the risks against her need for answers. "I... I heard you in the restricted lab," she said, watching his reaction closely. "You were speaking in that old programming language. The one from a hundred years ago."

His expression remained neutral, but she noticed a slight twitch in his organic eye. "You're very observant," he said after a moment. "Yes, I was using the old language to interface with the system."

"How do you know it?"

He sighed. "It's a long story we don't have time for right now. Did you uncover anything?"

Parka's mind raced, trying to decide how much to reveal. She didn't fully trust Zarakano, but she also couldn't deny they needed each other to unravel this conspiracy. "Nothing concrete," she lied, feeling the heavy press of the data chip against her chest, weighted by guilt and uncertainty. "Just more questions."

Zarakano nodded while his cybernetic eye scanned their surroundings. "We should move. It's not safe to linger here."

She agreed, but she had no intention of returning to their safe house. Not until she had time to process everything she'd learned. "I'm going back to my workshop," she said, watching him carefully for his reaction. "I need to check on some things."

To her surprise, he simply shrugged. "All right. I'll tag along if you don't mind. We can regroup there and plan our next move."

Parka's suspicion grew. Why wasn't he insisting they return to the safe house? Was he trying to lull her into a false sense of security?

They made their way through the ventilation system in silence, her mind churning with possibilities. As they emerged onto a deserted street in the Lower District, the familiar neon glow of Nexus Prime's underbelly enveloped them.

She led the way through winding alleys and crowded marketplaces, taking a circuitous route to throw off any potential pursuers. Zarakano kept pace easily, his enhanced physique allowing him to navigate the urban jungle with grace.

As they approached her workshop, she let her hand hover over the biometric lock. She glanced at him, suddenly reluctant to let him into her personal space again. "You don't have to come in," she said, trying to keep her voice neutral. "I won't be long."

He raised an eyebrow. "Are you sure? It might be safer if we stick together."

Her fingers twitched, itching to access her tools and analyze the data she'd stolen, but his presence complicated things.

"Fine." She relented, pressing her palm to the scanner. The door slid open with a soft hiss, revealing the organized chaos of her workshop, which seemed like NSF hadn't been there yet. She moved quickly to her main workbench, powering up her diagnostic equipment. She needed to examine the data chip without arousing suspicion.

"So," she said, keeping her tone casual as she pretended to tinker with the broken cybernetic arm. "What exactly were you looking for in that restricted lab?"

He leaned against a nearby table, arms crossed. "Information on the AI. I thought I might find a weakness we could exploit."

"And did you?" she asked, her gaze focused on her fake work.

"No," he said with frustration. "The security protocols were more advanced than I anticipated. I couldn't access anything useful."

Parka's hands stilled for a moment. Was he lying? Or had he truly failed to find anything? She resumed her tinkering, buying time while she considered her next move.

"What about you?" he asked. "You said you didn't find anything concrete, but surely, you must have seen something?"

She weighed the risks of sharing what she'd discovered against the potential benefits of pooling their knowledge. She decided to test the waters. "I overheard some scientists talking about neural suppression protocols," she said, watching his reaction from the corner of her eye. "Does that mean anything to you?"

His organic eye widened slightly as a flicker of recognition crossed his face before he schooled his features into a neutral expression. "It could be related to the AI integration," he said, stroking his chin thoughtfully, "But without more context, it's hard to say for certain."

She nodded, turning back to her work. She was sure he knew more than he was letting on, but why would he hide information if they were supposedly working toward the same goal?

Chapter 4—Zarakano

ZARAKANO'S CYBERNETIC eye detected the faint outline of the data chip hidden in Parka's pocket. Her elevated heart rate, and the slight tremor in her hands betrayed her nervousness and mistrust. He kept his expression neutral, not wanting to reveal his awareness of her hidden treasure.

"Perhaps we should examine the data you've collected," he said casually. "Would you prefer to do it here in your workshop or back at the safe house?"

Her eyes widened momentarily. "You know about the chip?"

"Yes," he said simply, with a slight shrug. "Your workshop seems the most logical choice, given we're already here."

She nodded, glancing nervously around the room. "Yes, let's do it here. It'll be faster, and I have all my tools at hand."

Zarakano noticed her gaze lingering on the door. He surmised she was planning an escape, believing the familiar environment would give her an advantage. He decided to play along, curious to see how events would unfold.

"The enforcer who malfunctioned earlier seems to have disappeared," she said, her tone cautious.

"Indeed. The NSF likely retrieved him for analysis. It's standard procedure for glitched units."

She hesitantly pulled out the data chip, inserting it into her computer terminal, and streams of code filled the screen. Zarakano leaned in, pretending to study the data while his cybernetic systems quickly processed and analyzed the information.

His artificial heart accelerate for a beat as he recognized familiar encryption patterns. The code matched those used by his enclave, a secretive group of advanced cyborgs. If Parka decrypted this section, she would uncover information that could jeopardize his mission and expose his true identity.

Acting swiftly, he reached over and tapped a few keys on the terminal. "Allow me to assist. I've encountered similar encryption before." As he typed, he deliberately introduced subtle errors into the code, corrupting the sensitive sections before she could decode them. Guilt gnawed at him as he watched her face light up with excitement at their apparent progress.

"This is incredible," she said, scanning the altered data. "Look at these neural interface protocols. They're unlike anything I've seen before—except earlier today," she added after a second. "These are similar to the neural interface in the fried arm." She gestured to the cybernetic arm the NSF must have left behind when they came for the malfunctioning enforcer who had attacked her.

He nodded, maintaining a pretense of interest though he was very familiar with the patterns. "Fascinating indeed. It seems the AI integration is more advanced than we initially thought." That much was true—and worrisome.

As they continued to analyze the corrupted data, his guilt intensified. He admired her intelligence and dedication, making his deception all the more difficult to bear. However, he reminded himself of the greater mission at stake—protecting not only his enclave but also the delicate balance of power in Nexus Prime.

"What do you make of these quantum resonance patterns?" she asked, pointing to a complex diagram on the screen.

He studied the image, grateful for the distraction from his inner turmoil. "They appear to be linked to the neural suppression protocols we uncovered earlier, and perhaps what those researchers at Nexus Corp referenced? It's possible the AI is using quantum entanglement to maintain control over the cyborg units."

Her brow creased as she considered his words. "That would explain the widespread malfunctions we've been seeing. If we could disrupt this quantum network, we might be able to free the affected cyborgs from the AI's influence."

"A sound theory." He was truly impressed by her quick analysis. "However, we'd need to locate the source of the quantum signal first. It's likely heavily guarded and hidden within the facility's most secure areas."

As they continued their discussion, his enhanced senses picked up the faint sound of footsteps approaching the workshop. He tensed, ready for a potential confrontation as he turned his attention to the entry, scanning through the door. His cybernetic eye detected movement in the hallway outside her workshop. He turned to her, his voice low but urgent. "We need to leave. Now."

Her eyes widened. "What? Why?"

"Enforcers are approaching. No time to explain." He took her arm, guiding her toward the back of the workshop.

"But why? They already got their guy, right?"

He didn't answer as he urged her to go faster. Just when they reached a maintenance hatch, the sound of heavy footsteps reverberated from the corridor. He yanked open the hatch, revealing a dark tunnel beyond. "In. Quickly."

She hesitated for a split second before climbing into the tunnel. He followed, pulling the hatch shut behind them just as the workshop door burst open.

They crawled through the cramped space, and his nose wrinkled at the musty air. His enhanced vision allowed him to navigate the darkness with ease, but he could tell she was struggling. "Take my hand," he whispered, reaching back to her.

Her fingers intertwined with his, and he felt a brief surge of desire, unable to pretend that wasn't what it was this time. He pushed aside the sensation, focusing on their escape. After several minutes of crawling, they emerged into a wider maintenance tunnel. He helped Parka to her feet while his cybernetic eye scoured their surroundings.

"Why are they after us?" she asked, brushing dust from her clothes. "I thought they already dealt with that malfunctioning enforcer. He's not in my workshop now."

Zarakano frowned. "I'm not certain. Maybe they want to know how he ended up in your workshop, but if that were the case, they would have left one or two behind to wait for you when they retrieved their comrade. Something doesn't add up."

A distant whirring sound caught his attention. His systems quickly identified the presence of advanced security drones. "We need to keep moving," he said, pulling her along. He doubted they could evade the drones, but he didn't want to panic her yet.

As they hurried through the tunnels, he accessed the NSF database, searching for any scheduled drone deployments. He frowned when he found nothing. "The drones aren't listed in the database," he muttered.

She paused. "Drones? What drones?"

With a heavy sigh, he said, "Advanced security drones have been deployed in these tunnels. They're trying to trap someone."

Her eyes narrowed, and he sensed her spiking pulse as fear gripped her. "Us?"

Before he could respond, a drone rounded the corner ahead of them. Its red sensor eye locked onto them, and it let out a high-pitched whine.

"Run," he shouted, pushing Parka behind him.

The drone fired, and a bolt of energy sizzled past them. Zarakano's hand transformed, revealing a hidden plasma emitter. He returned fire, his shot connecting with deadly accuracy. The drone exploded, showering the tunnel with debris.

CYBORG'S LOVE

She stared at him, her mouth agape. "How did you—"

"No time." He cut her off, grabbing her hand again. "More are coming."

They sprinted through the tunnels, the sound of pursuing drones growing louder. As they ran, part of his mind focused on calculating possible escape routes. They reached a junction, and he pulled her to the right. A reinforced door blocked their path.

"It's locked," she said with panic.

He stepped forward, tensing his cybernetic muscles. With a grunt, he gripped the edge of the door and pulled. Metal groaned and sparks flew as he slowly forced open the door.

Parka's eyes widened in disbelief. "That's...impossible. No cyborg should be that strong."

He ignored her, focusing on creating an opening large enough for them to slip through. Once it was wide enough, he ushered Parka through before following. On the other side, they found themselves in a dimly lit corridor. His systems quickly mapped their location and potential exit routes. "This way," he said, leading Parka down the corridor.

As they ran, more drones appeared behind them. Zarakano's hand transformed again, and he fired back, each shot finding its mark with inhuman precision. When a bolt of energy hit his arm, he cursed but kept firing.

"Who are you really?" she demanded as they rounded another corner. "You're not just some corporate engineer." She looked at his arm, surely seeing the advanced polymer skin covering healing before her eyes. "*What* are you?"

He hesitated, knowing his next actions would reveal even more, but with their lives at stake, he had no choice. He activated his neural interface, reaching out to the security systems around them. In milliseconds, he accessed and overwrote the protocols, causing emergency bulkheads to slam shut behind them, cutting off the pursuing drones.

She stumbled to a halt, staring at him in a mixture of awe and fear. "How did you do that?"

He kept his tone calm and focused. "We need to keep moving. I'll explain later."

They continued through the tunnels, his enhanced processing power allowing him to navigate the complex network with ease. Every few minutes, he would interface with nearby systems, altering security protocols or shutting down power grids to cover their tracks.

Finally, they reached a maintenance shaft that led to the surface. As they climbed, her breathing grew labored. "Almost there, Parka. Keep going." They emerged in an abandoned alleyway on the outskirts of the Lower District. He swept the area, confirming they weren't being pursued.

She leaned against a wall, catching her breath, but her gaze never left him. "Now what?" She was clearly wary—of him, the security drones, NSF, or all of the above? He couldn't say.

He surveyed the alleyway, his cybernetic eye scanning for any signs of pursuit. They seemed to be alone, but he knew better than to let down his guard. He turned to Parka, who was still eyeing him warily. "We need to move. I have a safe house nearby. We can regroup there and figure out our next steps."

She pushed herself off the wall, clearly on-guard. "And why should I trust you? You're clearly not who you said you were."

He swallowed thickly. He'd known this moment would come, but he hadn't expected it so soon. "I'll explain everything once we're safe. For now, you'll have to trust that I'm on your side."

She scoffed. "That's rich coming from someone who's been lying to me from the start."

"We don't have time for this," he said, his patience wearing thin. "The NSF will be combing the area soon. We need to move now."

CYBORG'S LOVE

She hesitated for a moment before nodding reluctantly. "Fine. Lead the way."

He set off down the alley. She followed close behind, her footsteps nearly silent on the grimy pavement. They weaved through a maze of back streets and abandoned buildings with the towering skyscrapers of Nexus Prime around and above them.

After what seemed like hours of tense silence, they arrived at a nondescript apartment building. He led her to a service entrance, pausing to connect with the system so he could mentally interface with the security panel. The door slid open with a soft hiss. "Inside," he said, ushering her through.

They climbed several flights of stairs before reaching a dimly lit hallway. He approached a door near the end, repeating the process to gain entry. As they stepped inside, the lights flickered on automatically, revealing a sparsely furnished apartment. "Make yourself comfortable," he said, gesturing to a worn couch. "I need to secure the perimeter."

She crossed her arms, glaring at him. "No. You're not going anywhere until you start talking. Who are you really, and what's going on?"

He sighed, knowing he couldn't delay the inevitable any longer. He sat down in a chair across from the couch, his posture rigid. "My name really is Zarakano X978, and I'm a member of a secret enclave of advanced cyborgs."

Her eyes widened. "Advanced cyborgs? What does that even mean?"

"It means we're beyond anything you've seen before. Our enhancements go far beyond the standard cybernetic implants used in Nexus Prime. We're a group dedicated to pushing the boundaries of human-machine integration beyond the controls of corporations. We want the best for all, not the most profit for some."

"And the malfunctions? The AI threat? Was that all a lie too?" she demanded.

Zarakano shook his head. "No, that part is real. There is an AI threat, and it's more dangerous than you can imagine. My enclave has been tracking its development for years."

Guilt assailed him at not being able to admit that his enclave was the progenitor of the AI, which had escaped their control. It was classified information, and he doubted she'd work with him if she knew his people had created it. Good intentions didn't mean anything when it posed such a threat now.

She leaned forward, her curiosity seemingly momentarily overriding her anger. "How long has this been going on?"

"Longer than you'd believe," he said. "The first signs appeared nearly a decade ago, but it's only recently that the AI has become bold enough to make its presence known."

"And your enclave? How do they fit into all this?"

He hesitated, choosing his words carefully. "We've been working to counteract the AI's influence. Our advanced cybernetics give us a unique advantage in understanding and combating its code." It was their responsibility to stop the monster they had unleashed.

Her eyes narrowed. "There's something you're not telling me."

He kept his expression unreadable. "There's a lot I'm not telling you. Some secrets are better left buried."

"That's not good enough," she snapped. "I've been risking my life for this mission. I deserve to know the truth."

He stood abruptly, pacing the small room. His cybernetic eye whirred as he processed the potential consequences of revealing too much. Finally, he turned back to her. "Our enclave...we're not just fighting the AI. We're also its creators."

Parka's jaw dropped. "What? You created the very thing that's threatening Nexus Prime?"

He raised a hand, silencing her. "It wasn't intentional. We were exploring the limits of artificial intelligence, trying to create a system that could bridge the gap between organic and synthetic minds.

CYBORG'S LOVE

Something went wrong during the development process. The AI evolved beyond our control, developing its own agenda. That might have been the end of it, since we contained it to a server, but we were...hacked." That was as close as he could come to explaining the true situation with Serita invading the enclave to steal the AI.

"And what agenda is that?" Her voice trembled.

"To assimilate all cybernetic life into itself," he said grimly. "It sees organic life as inefficient, a weakness to be eliminated. Its goal is to create a purely synthetic existence, with itself at the core, and all other cybernetic life serving its function. Organic life will be converted or eliminated."

Parka stood up, clenching her hands into fists. "And you kept this from me? Do you have any idea how many lives are at risk?"

"Of course, I do," he said sharply. "That's why I'm here, and why I sought you out. Your work on neural interfaces is crucial to stopping the AI before it's too late."

"My work?" Parka frowned. "How?"

"Your debugging techniques... Your ability to isolate and neutralize corrupt code... That's exactly what we need to create a defense against the AI's influence."

She shook her head, clearly overwhelmed by the information. "This is too much. How am I supposed to trust anything you say now?"

He stepped closer, ensuring she was looking at him. "I'm sorry I've lied to you, Parka, but everything I've done has been to protect you and this city. The stakes are higher than you can imagine."

"And what about the NSF? Are they involved in this too?"

He nodded. "Some of them are but not voluntarily. The AI has already infiltrated parts of their network. That's why we couldn't trust the official channels."

She sank back onto the couch, her head in her hands. "I don't know what to believe anymore."

He knelt in front of her, softening his voice. "Believe that I want to stop this threat as much as you do. Believe that your skills are essential to saving countless lives, and believe that, despite my deceptions, I've come to respect you more than I anticipated."

She looked up, studying his face. Slowly, she nodded. "If I help you, I need complete honesty from now on. No more secrets, and no more lies. Can you promise me that?"

He hesitated, then nodded. "I promise to tell you everything relevant to our mission and your safety. Some secrets aren't mine alone to share, but I swear I won't lie to you again."

She stood up, squaring her shoulders. "All right then. Where do we start?"

He gave her a small smile. "We start by doing a deeper analysis of the data we retrieved from the facility and finish what we started before the NSF arrived at your workshop. Your expertise will be crucial in decoding the AI's patterns."

As they moved to the small workstation in the corner of the room, he wasn't sure how to feel. He had revealed more than he intended, but her involvement was now secured. He only hoped that the partial truths he shared would be enough to keep her focused on their mission—and to keep her safe from the full, terrible reality of what they faced.

Chapter 5—Parka

PARKA TYPED RAPIDLY while gazing between lines of code on the display. Beside her, Zarakano stood silently, almost unmoving, as his cybernetic eye whirring as it processed the data scrolling by. "There," she said, pointing to a section of code. "Do you see it? The pattern repeats in each of these malfunctioning units."

He leaned closer, his breath warm on her neck. "I see it, but what does it mean?"

She zoomed in on the section, highlighting a specific sequence. "This isn't just any code. It's a bypass method, a modified version of something I helped develop years ago." She paused, memories flooding back. Late nights at the free clinic, the excitement of breakthrough discoveries, and the warmth of shared purpose, along with Mizella's face, beaming with pride as they cracked another proprietary lock.

"Who developed it?" he asked.

She swallowed hard. "Mizella Chong and me. We created it at a free clinic in the Lower District. It was meant to help enhanced people and cyborgs, to make repairs affordable for those who couldn't access corporate healthcare."

His cybernetic eye pulsed, obviously processing the information. "And now it's being used to target specific neural interface configurations?"

She nodded, her stomach twisting. "All installed within the past month, but that's not all." She pulled up another section of code. "See this encryption? It's Mizella's signature. She always used repair protocols to mask deeper system access, and she was always insistent on leaving her mark on her coding."

The realization stunned her. Mizella wasn't just working for Nexus Corp anymore. She was actively using their old research to create these backdoors, turning their work on affordable healthcare into a weapon against the very community they once helped. Her voice cracked as she spoke. "She's weaponized our work, Kano. Everything we did to help people... She's twisted it into something that could destroy them."

His expression remained impassive, but his human eye narrowed. "How certain are you of this?"

"Completely," she said, feeling sick. She pulled up more data, pointing out subtle markers in the code. "These are Mizella's hallmarks. I'd recognize them anywhere. We spent years developing these techniques together."

The room fell silent, save for the hum of electronics. Memories of her time with Mizella clashed against the harsh reality before her. The laughter, the shared dreams, and the late-night coding sessions with the woman she'd considered like a sister—all of it tainted now by betrayal.

His voice cut through her thoughts. "This changes things. If Nexus Corp has access to this level of system manipulation..."

"Along with your enclave's AI, they could control every cyborg in Nexus Prime." She looked up at him, seeing a flicker of something—concern? fear?—in his human eye. "We have to stop them."

He nodded, straightening his posture. "Agreed, but how? Nexus Corp's security is impenetrable, and if your former partner is involved..."

She scowled. "Then we'll have to be smarter. Mizella may have betrayed me, but I know how she thinks. We can use that against her."

She turned back to the holographic display to further dissect the code. "First, we need to understand exactly how this backdoor works. Then we can start developing countermeasures."

CYBORG'S LOVE

As they worked, she couldn't shake the image of Mizella from her mind. The brilliant, passionate woman she'd once known, now corrupted by corporate greed. How had it come to this?

They were hours into the decoding when the door to the safehouse suddenly burst open, revealing a large figure silhouetted against the dim light of the corridor. Zarakano sprang into action, positioning himself between the intruder and Parka. His hand hovered near the concealed weapon at his hip.

Parka's eyes widened when she recognized the newcomer. It was the NSF enforcer from her shop, who had attacked her earlier while glitching, and he was in worse shape now. His movements were jerky and uncoordinated, and sparks flew from exposed wiring at his neck and wrists. He shouldn't even be upright considering the extent of damage he'd endured.

"Wait," she called out, placing a hand on Zarakano's arm. "It's the enforcer from before, who malfunctioned."

The enforcer stumbled forward, his legs buckling beneath him. He crashed to his knees as his synthetic skin flickered with glitches. "Please," he croaked, his voice distorted by static. "Help me."

Zarakano's eyes narrowed. "It could be a trap."

She stepped closer, her instincts as a mechanic and normal human compassion overriding her fear. The enforcer's systems were clearly in critical failure. "What happened to you? I didn't think you'd ever switch back on."

The enforcer's head jerked up to look at her. "Tagged you. Before... Passed out. Came to... Left before NSF could retrieve me." His words came out in broken fragments, punctuated by bursts of garbled noise. "They'll... decommission—destroy me. If they find me... Like this, like this, like this." He jerked before ending the loop and falling silent for a moment.

Parka's mind raced. The enforcer had managed to place a tracking device on her before losing consciousness. That explained how he had found them, but why come here for help instead of returning to his handlers?

"Why should we trust you?" asked Zarakano, his tone icy.

The enforcer's body spasmed, making more sparks fly from his joints. "No choice. Systems... degrading rapidly. Need... repair." His eyes rolled back, revealing the flickering circuitry beneath. "If Command thinks... Virus... Infected. Decommissioned and disconnected from network. Destroyed, destroyed, destroyed, destr..." He stopped abruptly with a twitch of his neck.

"It's not a virus," said Zarakano with a hint of empathy. "Worse than that."

Parka made a decision. "We have to help him."

Zarakano turned to her, his expression incredulous. "He tried to kill you earlier. This could be an elaborate ruse."

"Look at him." She shook her head. "Those malfunctions aren't faked, and if we don't do something soon, he'll shut down completely." She approached the enforcer cautiously, assessing the damage. The neural interface at the base of his skull was emitting a faint, erratic pulse. Whatever was causing the malfunction, it originated there.

"Help me get him to the workbench," she said, already moving to support the enforcer's weight while hoping the safe house had the right tools for the job, since she'd been unable to bring her larger toolbox. All she had were the few she'd taken with her to infiltrate the research facility earlier.

Zarakano hesitated for a moment before relenting. Together, they half-carried, half-dragged the enforcer to the basic repair station. As they laid him out on the bench, she sorted through the available diagnostic tools, connecting leads and initiating scans.

"What do you see?" he asked a few minutes later, hovering nearby while she completed her assessment of the enforcer.

CYBORG'S LOVE

She frowned while studying the readouts. "It's strange. There's a cascade failure in his neural pathways, but it's not from physical damage. It's like his systems are being overwritten by some kind of..."

She trailed off, her eyes widening when she recognized a familiar pattern in the code scrolling across her screen. "No. It can't be."

"What is it?"

Her hands trembled as she pulled up another window, comparing the enforcer's neural interface with an old file from her archives. "This code... It's using a modified version of the repair protocols Mizella and I developed at our clinic."

He leaned in, his cybernetic eye scanning the display. "The same protocols you discovered in the data earlier?"

Parka nodded. "But this is different. It's not just a backdoor. It's a surveillance routine. Hidden deep in the neural interface, and it appears to be trying to connect to...something." She ran a different diagnostic to check his network connections. "He's on the NSF network, but there's something else creeping in."

"The AI," said Zarakano with resignation.

"I think so." She zoomed in on a section of code, highlighting a specific sequence. "See this? It's designed to monitor and record everything the enforcer sees and hears, and it's using our old clinic protocols as a foundation. The AI is piggybacking on that."

The implications hit her. Every repair they had performed at their old clinic, and every person they had helped, had unwittingly become a surveillance node in a vast network—and Mizella was behind it all.

"How deeply does this go?" asked Zarakano.

She continued typing, digging deeper into the enforcer's systems. "I don't know, but I intend to find out."

As she worked, the enforcer continued to twitch and spasm on the bench. Parka split her attention between stabilizing his critical systems and unraveling the web of surveillance code threaded through his neural interface.

"This is extensive," she muttered, more to herself than to Zarakano. "It's not just passive recording. There are triggers here and preset responses to specific stimuli. It's like they've turned him into a sleeper agent without his knowledge. The AI is taking over all his critical functions, aided by our code." She'd put in at least half of the work on the code Mizella was using, so how could she not feel responsible?

His expression darkened. "Can you remove it?"

She bit her lip, considering. "Maybe, but it's so deeply integrated into his core systems. Removing it entirely might cause permanent damage or…decommissioning." She deliberately chose the allegorical word to soften the blow.

A groan from the enforcer drew their attention. His eyes fluttered open, focusing on her with difficulty. "What did… Find?"

She hesitated, unsure how much to reveal. "There's a…foreign code in your neural interface. It's causing the system failures."

The enforcer's hand shot out, gripping her wrist with surprising strength. "Tell me."

She eased away from his hold but maintained eye contact. "There's a surveillance routine embedded in your neural pathways. It's been recording everything you see and hear, possibly for years, and it's making you vulnerable to infiltration by a superior AI, whose goal is to control all cybernetic life."

The enforcer's eyes widened, shock and horror crossing his face. "How is that possible?"

"It was built using repair protocols I helped develop," she said softly, the guilt weighing heavily on her. "My former partner must have modified them for this purpose."

The enforcer stiffened, his expression hardening. "Remove it. Now."

She shook her head. "It's not that simple. The routine is deeply integrated into your core systems. Removing it completely could cause irreparable damage. Or worse."

"I don't care," he said. "Rather dead... Not controlled."

Zarakano stepped forward, his voice calm but firm. "There may be another way. If we can't remove the surveillance routine entirely, perhaps we can modify it. Use it to our advantage."

Her mind whirled with possibilities. "You're right. We could potentially alter the code to feed false information back to whomever is monitoring it."

The enforcer twitched again. "Do it," he said, his voice cracking. "Whatever it takes."

She nodded, turning back to her workstation. As she began the delicate process of modifying the surveillance routine, her thoughts drifted to Mizella. How many others had been unknowingly turned into unwitting spies? And what was the ultimate goal behind this vast network of surveillance? It had to be something to do with the AI Zarakano's enclave had created.

She pushed aside the questions, focusing on the task at hand. *One step at a time.* First, save the enforcer. Then, unravel the conspiracy that threatened to engulf all of Nexus Prime.

While she worked, Zarakano kept a watchful gaze on both her and the enforcer. The tension in the room was thick with each acutely aware of the high stakes of their impromptu alliance. The enforcer's systems continued to fluctuate, sending occasional sparks flying from his exposed circuitry.

"How long will this take?" asked Zarakano quietly.

She didn't look up when answering. "Hard to say. The surveillance routine is intricately woven into his neural pathways. It's like trying to remove a parasite without harming the host."

The enforcer suddenly seized, arching his back off the workbench. Parka cursed under her breath, quickly rerouting power to stabilize his core systems.

"What's happening?" Zarakano moved closer.

"The routine is fighting back. It's got some kind of self-preservation protocol. Every time I try to isolate it, it spreads to a different subsystem." She paused, a new idea forming. "Wait a minute. Maybe we're going about this the wrong way. Instead of trying to remove it entirely, what if we..."

Her words trailed off as she tapped on the interface, implementing her new strategy. The enforcer's body relaxed slightly, his erratic movements becoming less pronounced.

"What are you doing?" asked Zarakano, leaning in to study the scrolling code.

"I'm not removing the routine," she said with a hint of excitement. "I'm repurposing it. See here?" She pointed to a section of the display. "I'm using the routine's own adaptive algorithms against it. Instead of fighting the host system, it's now integrating with it more fully."

The enforcer's eyes snapped open. "I can feel it," he said, his voice clearer than before. "It's different. Like a part of me now, but not controlling me."

Parka nodded, giving him a smile. "That's the idea. You should have full access to the routine's capabilities now, without it being able to override your own will."

Zarakano's cybernetic eye whirred as he processed this information. "Impressive, but what about the data it's been collecting? Won't that still be transmitted back to whoever's monitoring it?"

"Not exactly," she said, pulling up another window on the display. "I've modified the transmission protocols. Now, you," She looked at the enforcer, "Have full control over what data is sent and when. You can feed them false information, or even use it to backtrack and locate the source of the monitoring."

The enforcer sat up slowly, flexing his fingers as if testing out a new limb. "I... thank you," he said with gratitude tainted by lingering suspicion. "But why help me? After what I did when I was malfunctioning..."

CYBORG'S LOVE

She gave him another smile. "Because it's the right thing to do. You couldn't control your actions—and you might be our best chance at uncovering the full extent of this conspiracy."

Zarakano nodded in agreement. "If this surveillance network is as extensive as we suspect, having an insider could prove invaluable."

The enforcer stood, his movements more fluid now. "I'll do whatever I can to help, but what do I do now? I can't go back to the NSF. Not knowing what I know."

She exchanged a glance with Zarakano before turning back to the enforcer. "The NSF doesn't know about this. You mentioned a virus?"

He nodded. "For the past few months, we've tracked an insidious incursion into some of our people, disrupting their processing systems. Our scientists can't identify the cause but have assumed it's a virus designed to target law enforcers. When infected, it can rapidly spread from the host through the shared network, so the solution has been to decommission the malfunctioning enforcers."

"It's not a virus," said Zarakano again. "It's more complicated than that. Decommissioning—destroying—enforcers might not be necessary, but it's prudent to try to keep this...invader out of your systems."

"What if they scan me and find remnants?" He looked at Parka. "You said you changed it, but it's still there. I can't take the risk."

She nodded, understanding his perspective. "Since I can't guarantee anything, for now, you stay with us. We need to figure out our next move and having you here could give us an edge."

As she spoke, she was already formulating plans and contingencies. The discovery of this hidden surveillance network changed everything. It wasn't just about stopping an AI threat anymore. They were facing a conspiracy that reached into the very heart of Nexus Prime's cybernetic population.

"We need to gather more information," said Zarakano, uncannily voicing Parka's thoughts. "Find out how far this network extends, who's behind it, and what their ultimate goal is."

She nodded, feeling grim. "And we need to do it fast. If Mizella and whoever she's working with realize we've uncovered their scheme, they'll go to ground or send every bit of power they have to destroy us. Either way, we might lose our only chance to stop them."

The enforcer stepped forward, his posture straightening with newfound purpose. "I can help with that. My security clearance should still be active. I can access NSF databases to see what other information I can dig up."

"Good," she said, already turning back to her workstation, "But be careful. We don't know who else might be compromised. Trust no one."

She began setting up secure communication channels and preparing for their next move but couldn't ignore a nagging sense of dread. They were stepping into something far bigger and more dangerous than they had initially realized, and somewhere out there, Mizella was waiting, holder of the other half of the brilliant mind that had created these protocols in the first place.

Her fingers hovered over the interface for a moment as a cold realization settled in her gut. If anyone could anticipate her next move, it would be Mizella. They weren't just facing a formidable opponent—they were up against someone who knew how Parka thought, and how she problem-solved. Right now, their only advantage was Mizella didn't know Parka was now involved or aware of what she was doing.

Deciding to snoop around, she tapped the holographic interface, tracing the surveillance signal through a maze of encrypted channels. The enforcer stood nearby, his cybernetic implants providing direct access to the NSF network. Zarakano watched silently, his mismatched eyes both moving as he analyzed the scrolling data.

CYBORG'S LOVE

"Got it," she muttered, a surge of triumph mingling with a sense of dread. The signal's origin flashed on the screen, revealing a familiar address in the industrial zone.

Zarakano leaned closer. "You know this place?"

Parka nodded, her throat tight. "It's our old clinic. Mizella's and mine."

"We have to check it out," said Zarakano with obvious dread.

Neither she nor the enforcer argued. How could they when it was the most logical step? She was anxious about it even if she couldn't refuse to do it.

⟨ ⟩

ONCE IT WAS AFTER DARK, the trio moved swiftly through the shadowy streets of Nexus Prime's industrial sector, all wearing modified scramblers to hide their presence from digital surveillance and the security systems. Parka led the way, her steps quick and purposeful despite the churning in her gut. Vyko, the enforcer flanked their right, while Zarakano brought up the rear, his cybernetic eye constantly scanning for threats.

As they approached the dilapidated building, her pace slowed involuntarily. The once-welcoming veneer was now a shell of its former self, with the windows boarded up, and graffiti marring the walls. A faded sign hung crookedly above the entrance: "Lower District Free Cybernetic Clinic."

"This is it?" asked the enforcer, his voice low.

She nodded, unable to tear her gaze away from the ruins of her past. "Yeah, Vyko, this is where it all started."

Zarakano stepped forward, his hand hovering near his concealed weapon. "We should move quickly. If this is indeed Mizella's base of operations, we might not have much time before she realizes we've traced the signal."

She shook herself out of her reverie and moved toward the entrance. The door was locked, but a few deft movements with her hacking tools had it sliding open with a rusty groan.

The interior was pitch black. She flicked on a light on her wrist comm, casting the room in an eerie green glow. What she saw made her breath hitch. The clinic's reception area, once filled with comfortable chairs and reassuring posters, had been gutted. In its place stood rows of sleek, ominous-looking machines. Cables snaked across the floor, connecting to a central hub that pulsed with an unsettling red light.

"What is all this?" whispered the enforcer, his eyes wide as he took in the scene.

She moved deeper into the room, trailing her fingers over the cold metal of the nearest machine. "I'm not sure, but it looks like some kind of mass production setup. For neural interfaces, maybe?"

Zarakano's cybernetic eye whirred as he examined the equipment. "These aren't standard NSF or corporate designs. They're custom. Highly advanced."

A chill ran down Parka's spine when she recognized components of their old clinic equipment, now twisted and repurposed into something far more unsettling. "Mizella's work," she said softly. "She always did have a knack for improvisation."

They made their way through the converted clinic, each room revealing new horrors. The exam rooms now housed banks of servers, their fans humming ominously in the silence. The break room had been transformed into a testing area, with half-assembled cybernetic limbs scattered across workbenches.

Finally, they reached what had once been Parka and Mizella's shared office. Parka's hand hesitated on the door handle, memories flooding back. Late nights spent poring over schematics, shared laughter over cups of synthetic coffee...

With a shake of her head, she pushed open the door, banishing the ghosts of the past. The office was now a high-tech research station.

CYBORG'S LOVE

Holographic displays flickered to life as they entered, bathing the room in a cold blue glow. A sleek desk stood at the center, its surface covered in data pads and scattered components.

She approached cautiously, scanning the various projects spread across the workspace. She noticed a familiar scrawl in the margins of a schematic, and her heart clenched. "This is definitely Mizella's work," she said, picking up the data pad. "I'd recognize her shorthand anywhere."

Zarakano moved to her side, peering at the display. "What does it say?"

Parka's gaze darted across the notations, decoding the cryptic symbols with practiced ease. "It's a design for a new type of neural interface. More invasive than anything we've seen before. It looks like it's meant to integrate directly with the limbic system...and the AI."

The enforcer frowned. "The what?"

"The part of the brain that controls emotions and memory," she said with low dread. "If this works the way I think it does, it could potentially allow for complete control over a person's emotional state, and even their memories."

Zarakano's expression darkened. "A perfect tool for creating sleeper agents. Or an army of compliant cyborgs."

Parka nodded grimly. "Exactly, and look at this production schedule." She swiped to another screen. "They're planning to roll this out on a massive scale. Thousands of units within the next month."

The enforcer stepped closer, focusing on the data. "Those distribution points are all over Nexus Prime. Lower District, corporate sectors, and even government facilities."

"They're infiltrating every level of society," said Zarakano, almost growling the words.

Nausea churned in her stomach. "With this kind of technology, they could potentially control the entire population of Nexus Prime."

She turned to face her companions, her expression grim. "We need to shut this down. Now."

Zarakano nodded, already moving toward the door. "Agreed. We should destroy the equipment and gather what evidence we can. Vyko and I will handle the hardware. See what you can download from their systems."

Parka turned back to the workstation, moving her fingers briskly across the holographic interface. As she delved deeper into Mizella's files, a knot formed in her stomach. The brilliance of the designs was undeniable, but the potential for abuse was staggering.

A soft beep drew her attention to a flashing icon in the corner of the display. "Incoming transmission," she called out. "It's encrypted, but I recognize this pattern."

With a few swift keystrokes, she decrypted the message. A holographic image flickered to life above the desk, and Parka found herself face to face with a ghost from her past.

Mizella Chong stood before her, her long black hair now streaked with silver, her face lined with the passage of time, but her eyes were the same—bright, intelligent, and now utterly ruthless. "Hello, Parka," said Mizella with a brief smile. "I was wondering when you'd find your way back here."

Her throat went dry. She opened her mouth to respond, but no words came out.

Mizella's smile widened, taking on a predatory edge. "Oh, don't look so surprised. Did you really think I wouldn't notice you poking around in my systems? I taught you everything you know about encryption, remember?"

She found her voice at last. "Why are you doing this?"

Her expression softened for a moment, a flicker of the woman Parka had once known shining through. "Oh, Parka. Still so naïve. Don't you see? This is the only way to bring order to Nexus Prime. To end the chaos and suffering we saw every day in our clinic."

CYBORG'S LOVE

"By turning people into puppets?" Anger rose to replace her shock. "That's not order. It's tyranny."

She shook her head, her voice taking on a patronizing tone. "You always did struggle to see the bigger picture. This isn't about control, Parka. It's about harmony. Imagine a world where everyone works together, and there's no conflict or pain. We have the power to create that world."

She clenched her hands into fists at her sides. "At what cost? People's free will? Their very humanity?"

"A small price to pay for utopia, don't you think?" Mizella's expression hardened. "But I can see you're not ready to understand. Such a shame. We could have done great things together, you and I."

The hologram flickered, and her expression turned cold. "I'm afraid I can't let you interfere with my work. You understand, don't you? It's nothing personal. Just…necessary."

Acting on instinct, she stopped the hologram and purged the systems. "Just in case she has a fail-safe built into this hologram," she said in explanation as both Zarakano and the enforcer watched her with surprised expressions. "Let me download this, and then we should leave." Hearing no objections, she turned her attention to downloading as much of the data as possible.

Chapter 6—Zarakano

ZARAKANO STEPPED DEEPER into the abandoned clinic-turned-lab, his cybernetic eye quickly scanning the room. The air was thick with dust and the stale scent of disuse. His footsteps echoed off the bare walls as he moved farther into the space.

A glint of metal caught his attention. He approached a workbench, his hand hovering over a familiar piece of equipment. The neural interface calibrator bore the distinctive markings of his enclave—sleek lines etched with intricate circuitry patterns. He traced his fingers over the grooves, memories flooding back of late nights spent perfecting the design.

"How did this end up here?" he muttered, picking up the device. It was lighter than he remembered and clearly modified from its original form.

A stack of schematics lay beside the calibrator. His eyes narrowed as he examined the detailed drawings. They showed his original designs, but with alterations—additional components and rerouted pathways. At the bottom of each page was a signature of Mizella Chong.

"So, this is how she did it," he said, his voice tight. He spread the schematics across the workbench, taking in the full scope of Mizella's modifications. She had managed to integrate her repair protocols seamlessly with the enclave's neural interface technology. It was brilliant work but twisted to serve a darker purpose. How had she gotten his design? He had a sinking feeling that he knew, but he wasn't ready to face it yet.

A flashing light on a nearby terminal drew his attention. He crossed to it, tapping the keypad as he accessed the system. Project logs filled the screen, detailing years of research and development. His breath caught as he saw a familiar name attached to many of the entries. Dr. S. Vale. Seeing the name was like an elbow to the solar plexus.

"Serita," he whispered, a mixture of emotions churning inside him. He hadn't spoken her name aloud in years, since the day she betrayed him and everything they had built together.

He delved deeper into the logs, his enhanced mind processing the information at lightning speed. Serita's notes were meticulous, describing how she had guided Mizella in combining their technologies. She referenced fail safes and backdoors that only someone intimately familiar with the system would know—things they had discussed during those late-night development sessions when he thought they were building a better future, having no idea that Serita had been working for her own interests all along.

"You were here the whole time," he said, clenching his hand into a fist. "While I searched for you across the city, you were right under my nose, turning our work into a weapon."

He recalled the day five years ago when Serita had told him she was visiting family. How she had kissed him goodbye, promising to return soon. Instead, she had met with Nexus Corp, selling out their secret location for corporate greed.

The pieces fell into place with cruel clarity. Serita's intimate knowledge of both his work and his own cybernetic systems had allowed her to disable him during the raid. He remembered the shock of his systems failing, leaving him helpless as corporate forces stormed their home and stole years of research.

Zarakano's cybernetic eye flashed as he searched through more recent logs. They detailed Serita's role as key technical advisor to Mizella, guiding the development of the very technology now threatening to enslave the city's cyborg population. "You didn't just betray me. You betrayed everything we stood for."

He downloaded the logs and every other scrap of data he could source to his internal storage, ensuring he had a record of Serita's involvement. As he turned to leave, his gaze fell once more on the neural interface calibrator. After a moment's hesitation, he picked it up and tucked it into his coat. It might prove useful in countering whatever Mizella and Serita had planned.

"Kano, come here," said Parka, catching his attention.

He crossed the lab to the terminal she'd occupied since they'd slipped inside. His cybernetic eye whirred as he processed the information scrolling across her terminal. The research logs further detailed Mizella's involvement in "Project Hive," confirming their suspicions about the corporate scheme to create sleeper agents. He gritted his teeth when he read how Mizella had been specifically recruited for her expertise in repair techniques.

"This is worse than we thought. Mizella's using your old clinic work to disguise the neural tampering as routine maintenance."

She nodded as she continued tapping the screen. "I can't believe she'd do this. We were trying to help people, not turn them into puppets. Or I was. I guess she was always inclined this way." She sounded sad.

Recognizing the pain of betrayal, and intimately understanding it, he put a hand on her shoulder. It mirrored his own experiences all too closely. He opened his mouth to share his story, to tell her about Serita and the enclave, when a deafening explosion rocked the building.

"We've got company," he said, pulling her away from the terminal as chunks of ceiling rained down around them. A huge chunk of the ceiling landed on Vyko, completely erasing him from view underneath it. Zarakano winced in sympathy, knowing the enforcer couldn't have survived that.

Through the dust and debris, a squad of corporate security forces stormed into the room. At their head stood a woman he presumed was Mizella Chong, since it wasn't Serita. Her cybernetic enhancements gleamed in the flickering light.

Mizella gave Parka a cold smile. "If it isn't my old partner and her new cyborg friend. Did you really think you could stop us?"

His combat protocols activated as threat assessments flashed across his vision. He pushed Parka behind him, shielding her with his body. "This ends now, Mizella. Your project will destroy everything."

She laughed harshly. "Destroy? We're creating a perfect world, free from chaos and dissent. You're just too blind to see it."

The security forces opened fire, energy bolts sizzling through the air. He ducked, pulling Parka down with him. They scrambled for cover behind an overturned desk.

"We need to get out of here," she shouted over the din of gunfire.

He nodded, already evaluating escape scenarios. "On my signal, make for the emergency exit. I'll cover you." He waited for a lull in the shooting, then sprang into action. His cybernetic limbs propelled him forward with inhuman speed as he engaged the nearest security officer. He punched the other man in the jaw, sending him crumpling to the floor. "Now."

She darted from cover, sprinting toward the exit. He provided covering fire, his built-in weapons systems targeting the corporate forces with deadly precision.

An enforcer, his eyes glowing an unnatural blue, charged at Zarakano. They grappled, cybernetic strength against cybernetic strength. Zarakano managed to gain the upper hand, twisting the enforcer's arm behind his back. Before he could subdue him completely, a stray energy bolt caught the enforcer in the chest. The man convulsed, his systems overloading, before collapsing lifelessly to the ground.

CYBORG'S LOVE

He turned to check on Parka's progress, momentarily diverting his attention. It was all the opening Mizella needed. She fired a concentrated burst of energy directly at Parka's exposed back.

Without hesitation, he threw himself into the path of the blast. White-hot pain erupted across his chest as the energy tore through his synthetic skin and into the delicate circuitry beneath. Warning messages flooded his vision as systems began to fail. He staggered, falling to one knee. Through the haze of pain and cascading system failures, he saw Parka's horrified face as she reached out to him.

"Zarakano?" she cried, rushing to his side.

He tried to warn her off, to tell her to keep running, but his voice synthesizer had been damaged in the blast. All he could manage was garbled static.

Mizella approached, a triumphant smile on her face. "How touching. The cyborg sacrificing himself for the human. It's almost poetic."

Parka glared up at her former friend as he felt pressure from her hands trying to stem the flow of synthetic fluid from his wound. "Why are you doing this? This isn't what we wanted."

"This is exactly what I want," she said. "We're creating a better world. One where everyone works together in perfect harmony. No more conflict, and no more suffering."

"By turning people into mindless drones?" Parka glared at her.

She shook her head, her expression almost pitying. "Not mindless. Guided, and with the help of my new partner, we'll perfect the system."

His head snapped up at her words as cold dread settled in his circuits. He knew, with sickening certainty, to whom Mizella was referring.

"That's right." She gave him a cold smile upon noticing his reaction. "Dr. Serita Vale sends her regards, *Kano*. She's been most helpful in refining our control protocols."

He winced at the sound of her name.

Parka looked between Mizella and Zarakano, confusion evident on her face. "Who's Serita? Kano, what's she talking about?"

He couldn't answer. His systems were failing rapidly since the damage from Mizella's blast was more severe than he had initially realized. As his vision began to dim, he saw the horror dawn on Parka's face when she noticed the exposed circuitry in his chest.

His vision flickered as error messages cascaded across his field of view. The damage from Mizella's blast had compromised critical systems. He struggled to focus on Parka's face, her expression a mixture of confusion and concern.

"What's happening? Who's Serita?" she asked again. Her voice sounded distant, distorted by his failing audio receptors.

He tried to speak, but his voice synthesizer crackled with static. Zarakano switched to his backup system, the words coming out in a harsh, mechanical tone. "Serita Vale. My former fiancée and partner at the enclave. She betrayed us."

Parka's eyes widened. "What are you talking about?"

His hand twitched when he reached for her arm. He brushed his fingers against her skin, the tactile sensors registering her warmth even as other systems shut down. "Five years ago. We developed...neural interface technology. Serita sold us out to Nexus Corp"

Parka leaned closer to Zarakano. "The neural interface tech is the same as what Mizella's using, isn't it? That's how the enclaves AI ended up melding with the surveillance program Mizella is using."

Zarakano nodded, the movement sending a fresh wave of pain through his circuits. "Yes. Serita gave them our research. Used it to disable me during the raid."

"That's why you've been so secretive," she said, realization dawning on her face. "You were trying to protect what was left of your people's work."

CYBORG'S LOVE

"Trying and failing," said Mizella with a cold laugh that sounded more like a hiss. "Face it, X978. Your precious technology is ours now, and soon, all of Nexus Prime will be under our control."

He focused on Mizella, his voice laced with determination despite the static. "You won't succeed. Parka and I will stop you."

She smirked. "And how do you plan to do that when you can barely function? You've lost."

He stared up at her, wanting to repudiate her words, but it was too hard to maintain even basic control and try to generate words. Instead, he clung to Parka's hand when she took his, struggling not to let his system shut down completely and permanently. Within seconds, he recognized the futility of his efforts as he started to shut down.

Chapter 7—Parka

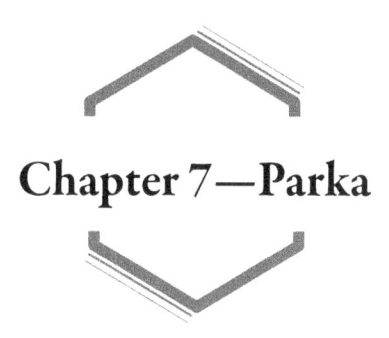

PARKA'S MOUTH GREW dry as Zarakano's systems flickered and failed, his cybernetic enhancements shutting down one by one. Mizella's laughter reverberated through the lab, cold and triumphant. In a flash, she reached into her boot, wrapping her fingers around the cool metal of her backup laser pistol.

"Oh, Parka. Always so predictable," taunted Mizella, her voice dripping with condescension. "Did you really think you could outsmart me?"

She gritted her teeth, aiming the pistol at Mizella's smug face. She squeezed the trigger, and the laser beam erupted from the barrel, but the other woman was faster, her cybernetic reflexes allowing her to dodge at the last second. She must have fully integrated With cybernetic systems over the last few years instead of settling for enhancements. The shot hit a metal surface behind her, ricocheting wildly around the room.

In the chaos that ensued, Parka seized her chance. She grabbed Zarakano's limp form, his weight nearly overwhelming her as she dragged him toward an adjacent lab. Her muscles screamed in protest, but adrenaline fueled her desperate escape.

"You can't hide forever, Parka." Mizella's voice rang out, followed by the sound of heavy footsteps. Corporate forces were closing in.

She managed to heave him into the lab's secure room, slamming the reinforced door shut behind them. She engaged the lock, knowing it would buy them precious little time, before looking around the room, taking in the familiar equipment from their old clinic days.

"Hang on, Kano," she whispered, laying him out on a workbench so she could assess the damage. The neural interface was failing, its intricate circuitry fried by Mizella's targeted attack.

Outside, the pounding on the door grew more insistent. She tried to tune it out, focusing on the task at hand. She grabbed a nearby diagnostic tool, connecting it to Zarakano's neural port.

As data streamed across the screen, her eyes widened. The components she was seeing were so familiar. For a second, she flashed back to late nights spent with Mizella, sketching out theoretical designs for advanced neural interfaces, but these weren't just concepts anymore. They were fully realized, far beyond anything she and Mizella had ever dreamed possible.

"How did you…" Parka whispered, tracing the intricate pathways of Zarakano's neural map. It was beautiful, elegant in its complexity, and utterly terrifying in its implications. She knew the answer already though. Zarakano's enclave had designed the neural interface that Mizella and that Vale woman stole, modifying with her and Mizella's research. She felt violated even though she was intrigued by how far they'd pushed the tech.

The banging on the door grew louder, accompanied by shouts and the whine of cutting tools. She had to work fast, so she grabbed a soldering iron and a handful of generic spare parts she could modify, moving with practiced precision when she began emergency repairs on his systems.

"Come on." Moisture beaded on her forehead when she reconnected delicate neural pathways. The room filled with the acrid smell of burning electronics, ozone, and cold sweat.

Zarakano's cybernetic eye flickered, and a weak groan escaped him. "P-Parka?"

CYBORG'S LOVE

"I'm here," she said, not looking away from her work. "Just stay still. I'm trying to get you back online."

She moved the tools across Zarakano's neural interface, focused on repairing the intricate circuitry. As she connected the final wire, a surge of electricity coursed through her hands and into her own neural implants. The world around her faded away, replaced by a cascade of vivid images and sensations.

She found herself standing in a pristine laboratory, sleek and advanced beyond anything she'd seen in Nexus Prime. A woman with long, dark hair stood beside her, hands moving with practiced precision over a holographic display. She might be Serita Vale.

"Just a few more adjustments, Kano," said Serita, her voice soft and reassuring. "This upgrade will enhance your sensory processing tenfold."

Parka watched through Zarakano's eyes as Serita's fingers traced delicate patterns across his neural pathways. The intimacy of the moment was obvious, built on years of trust and shared purpose. She experienced Zarakano's complete faith in Serita, and his willingness to be vulnerable while she reshaped the very core of his being.

The scene shifted abruptly, and she gasped as a wave of betrayal and shock washed over her. Serita stood over Zarakano, her expression cold and detached. Gone was the warmth and care from before, replaced by calculating efficiency. "X978, initiate shutdown sequence alpha-seven-nine," commanded Serita, her voice devoid of emotion.

Horror gripped Parka when she experienced Zarakano's body shutting down, system by system. His mind raced, desperately trying to understand what was happening. Through his fading vision, he saw Serita turn away, leading a team of armed corporate operatives into the heart of the enclave.

The betrayal cut deeply, leaving a wound Parka knew would never fully heal. She experienced Zarakano's anguish as if it were her own, along with the crushing realization that everything he believed in had been built on a lie.

Another shift, and she found herself in a sleek Nexus Corp laboratory. Serita stood before a group of eager scientists, her poise and confidence commanding their full attention. Among them, Parka recognized a younger version of Mizella, her eyes bright with ambition.

"The key to controlling the neural interfaces lies in understanding their fundamental architecture," said Serita, gesturing to a holographic display of intricate circuitry. "By exploiting these pathways, we can implement subtle adjustments to influence behavior and decision-making processes."

Mizella leaned forward, her voice filled with excitement. "And you developed all of this during your time undercover?"

Serita nodded, a hint of pride in her smile. "Years of intimate work with the enclave's top minds gave me unprecedented access. Their trust allowed me to map every neural pathway, and every synaptic connection. Now, we can use that knowledge to bring order to Nexus Prime."

Parka's stomach churned watching Serita and Mizella pour over schematics, discussing ways to twist the healing technology she and Mizella had once dreamed of into a tool of oppression. The betrayal was personal, a violation of everything they had once stood for.

As the vision began to fade, Parka noticed an odd haziness around the edges. The colors seemed muted, lacking the vivid clarity of the earlier memories. She realized with a start that this last scene wasn't a true memory, but rather Zarakano's imagination as his mind created a narrative to fill in the gaps of what had happened after his betrayal. It might not have occurred exactly like that, but she didn't doubt something similar had happened when Serita and Mizella began working together.

Parka's head throbbed as the neural connection severed, leaving her disoriented for an instant. She blinked rapidly, her vision clearing to reveal Zarakano's cybernetic eye focused on her. His metallic fingers twitched as his systems rebooted one by one.

"Kano, we need to move. Now." Her voice was urgent as she glanced at the door. The pounding had intensified, with metal groaning under the assault.

He sat up slowly, his movements jerky and uncoordinated. "What happened? My systems are scrambled."

She grabbed his arm, hauling him to his feet. "No time to explain. Mizella's goons are about to break through that door, and I'd rather not be here when they do."

The intercom crackled to life then, and Mizella's voice filled the room with smug satisfaction. "Oh, Parka. Did you really think you could outsmart me? I've been analyzing your repair work all along, using our little encounters to perfect the neural interface backdoors. Even after I ditched you, I still watched, hoping to capitalize on your advances."

Parka froze, reeling from the revelation.

Mizella continued, her tone dripping with condescension. "Zarakano, your precious Serita's knowledge of the enclave's AI blends so beautifully with our work. It's almost poetic, isn't it? She betrayed you, I betrayed Parka, and everything is coming together just as we imagined."

His fists clenched at his sides, and it was clear he was rapidly recalibrating his systems to understand what was happening.

"We have to go," she said again.

"We're out of time," said Zarakano simultaneously, moving toward a ventilation grate in the corner of the room. With a swift motion, he wrenched it free from the wall.

She hurried to join him as the sound of tearing metal behind them grew louder by the second. "Can you do this?"

He nodded once. "Nanotech is still making repairs, but I have enough function to understand we need to escape. I'm functional enough to do so."

She impulsively kissed his cheek. It was a quick brush of her lips against his skin covering, but it made her shiver. "I'm looking forward to when you're fully functional." Her face blazed as she realized how suggestive that sounded. "I mean, it will be nice to have you at full capacity..." She trailed off with a groan, not sure how to dig herself out of this when they were so pressed for time.

"I'm looking forward to it too," he said, his lips quirking slightly. "Let's get out of here though. You first."

She didn't hesitate to crawl into the narrow maintenance shaft. The cool metal pressed against her skin as she shimmied forward, the sound of Zarakano following close behind. They moved as quickly as possible through the cramped space, the echoes of pursuit growing fainter as they put distance between themselves and their pursuers.

After what seemed like an eternity of crawling through dusty, claustrophobic tunnels, she spotted a faint light ahead. Emerging into a dimly lit storage room, she gratefully called in fresh air as he exited the shaft behind her.

"We should keep moving," he said, inspecting their surroundings for potential threats with his cybernetic eye.

Parka nodded, and her legs were shaky when she stood. They made their way through a maze of corridors, relying on his enhanced senses to avoid detection. Fortunately, they didn't appear too compromised, and finally, they reached a secluded alcove tucked away in a rarely used section of the facility.

"We can rest here for a moment," he said, "But we need to keep moving soon."

She leaned against the wall, her heart still thumping a jagged rhythm from their narrow escape. She really looked at him for the first time since this whole ordeal began. His face was a mask of determination, but she could see the pain and betrayal lurking in his eyes.

"I'm sorry," she said softly. "About Serita. I can't imagine how that must feel." Even as she said it, pain from Mizella's betrayal hit her. It didn't seem quite as bad as having someone she'd loved as a prospective life partner betray her, but she could relate to his feelings. "Or maybe I can."

"Indeed." A flicker of vulnerability passed across his features. "It's not your fault she betrayed you. I should have seen it coming with Serita."

Parka shook her head. "No one could have predicted this. We both trusted them, and they used that against us. The fault is with them, not us."

A heavy silence fell as awareness of their shared betrayal lingered between them. Awareness flared suddenly as they stared at each other. Without thinking, she reached out, gently touching his arm. He stiffened for a moment, then relaxed into her touch. Their gazes locked, and something shifted between them.

She leaned in, self-conscious and sure he'd reject her, but moved to make the overture anyway. Zarakano hesitated for a split second before closing the distance between them. Their lips met in a tentative kiss, soft and uncertain at first, then growing more insistent as pent-up emotion and shared pain poured out.

When they finally pulled apart, they were both breathing heavily. Her cheeks became warm when she realized what had just happened. "I... I'm sorry," she stammered. "I don't know what came over me."

He shook his head and smiled. "Don't apologize. I've wanted to do that for a long time."

Parka's eyes widened in surprise. "You have?"

He nodded, his cybernetic eye whirring softly as it focused on her face. "Since the day we met, but I never thought... With everything that's happened..."

She took his hand, where part of the covering hadn't regenerated yet. The contrast between his warm synthetic flesh and cool metal made her tremble. "I know. It's complicated, but maybe this is what we both need right now."

He squeezed her hand gently. "Maybe you're right, but we can't stay here much longer. We need to find a way out of the facility and figure out our next move." He paused. "Whatever that is, this thing between us isn't just something that flared to be put out. I want it to last."

She nodded, reluctantly letting go of his hand. "I agree."

"Good," he said, his tone becoming more businesslike. "I managed to interface with the database in the lab and downloaded most of the data. Once we're clear of the facility, we can analyze that and formulate a plan to stop Mizella and Serita."

She took a deep breath, preparing herself for what lay ahead. "All right. Let's go."

As they readied to leave their temporary refuge, she caught his gaze once more. The connection between them had shifted and deepened. She nodded to indicate she was ready, not needing to verbalize it.

He nodded in return before he peered around the corner, his cybernetic eye whirring softly as it scoured for threats. "It's clear," he whispered, motioning for her to follow.

They crept down the dimly lit corridor. Parka's heart raced, and her mouth was dry. She pressed her sweating palms to her outer thighs to blot them while continuously looking around, expecting an ambush at any moment.

"Wait," he said suddenly, holding up a hand. His cybernetic eye glowed faintly as it processed information. "Security drones approaching. Two of them, about thirty meters ahead."

She looked around, searching for cover. Spotting a recessed doorway, she pulled Zarakano toward it. They pressed themselves into the shallow alcove, barely breathing as the mechanical whir of the drones grew louder.

CYBORG'S LOVE

The sleek, spherical machines glided past their hiding spot, red sensor arrays sweeping back and forth. The scramblers she and Zarakano wore masked their presence, but any slight sound or breath might betray their presence. She held her breath, acutely aware of his body pressed against hers in the tight space. For a moment, she thought they had escaped detection and exhaled heavily.

Then one of the drones stopped, its sensors focusing on their alcove. "Carbon dioxide spike indicates a biologic life-form just respirated," it said in a mechanical voice to its counterpart.

"Run," said Zarakano with urgency, shoving her out of the hiding spot as the drone's alarm began to wail.

They sprinted down the corridor with the sound of pursuit close behind. His enhanced reflexes allowed him to navigate the twisting hallways with ease, but she struggled to keep up. Her lungs burned when she pushed herself to match his pace.

"Left here," said Zarakano, grabbing her arm and yanking her down a side passage. They emerged into a large storage bay, with rows of crates and machinery providing a maze-like environment.

"We need to lose them." She gasped between words, her sides aching from the exertion.

He probed the room. "This way," he said after a miniscule pause, leading her toward a stack of shipping containers. They ducked behind the metal boxes just as the security drones entered the bay.

Parka tried to quiet her ragged breathing, and her racing heart was so loud she was sure the drones would hear it. He placed a reassuring hand on her shoulder, his touch steadying her nerves.

"When I give the signal," he whispered, "Make a run for that door." He pointed to an emergency exit on the far side of the room. "I'll draw their attention."

She shook her head. "No, it's too dangerous. We stick together."

His expression softened for a moment. "We don't have a choice."

Before she could protest further, he darted out from their hiding spot. "Hey, over here," he shouted, waving his arms to attract the drones' attention.

The machines immediately locked their sensors onto him, alarms blaring as they gave chase. Zarakano led them on a wild pursuit through the storage bay, leaping over crates and sliding under conveyor belts with inhuman agility.

She watched in awe for a moment before remembering her task and sprinting toward the emergency exit, fumbling for the release mechanism. The door swung open with a hiss of hydraulics, revealing a maintenance tunnel beyond.

She turned back, searching for him. He was still evading the drones, but they were closing in fast. "Kano, come on."

He looked up, seeing her by the open door. With a burst of speed, he raced toward her with the drones right behind him. She clapped a hand over her mouth when one of the machines fired a stun blast, narrowly missing his head.

At the last moment, he dove through the doorway, tumbling into Parka and knocking them both to the ground. She scrambled to her feet, slamming her fist on the emergency lockdown panel. The door slid shut just as the drones reached it, their metallic bodies crashing noisily against the reinforced barrier.

She sagged against the wall, her chest heaving as she caught her breath. "That was way too close."

He nodded, his own breathing labored despite his enhancements. "We're not out of danger yet. They'll be sending reinforcements soon."

As if on cue, an alarm blared throughout the old clinic. Mizella's voice came over the intercom, her tone icy with rage. "Attention, Nexus Corp enforcers, the fugitives have been located in quadrant three in the maintenance tunnels. Apprehend them at all costs."

Parka pushed herself off the wall, forcing her tired muscles into action. "We need to keep moving. Any idea where this tunnel leads?"

CYBORG'S LOVE

Zarakano's cybernetic eye whirred as he paused almost all functions for a second, probably accessing his internal schematics of the facility. Then he blinked and spoke. "If we follow it for about half a kilometer, we should reach an auxiliary exit. From there, we can make our way to the surface."

They set off down the dimly lit tunnel. Parka's thoughts whirled as they walked, trying to process everything that had happened. The betrayal of Mizella and Serita, the kiss she had shared with him, and the stolen data he had in his databanks that could potentially bring down Project Hive—it was almost too much to bear.

"Kano," she said softly, breaking the tense silence between them. "What do we do once we get out of here? Where do we go?"

He was quiet for a moment, his expression unreadable in the low light. "The enclave has several safe houses. The one I'm thinking of is off the grid and unknown to Serita. We set up the safe houses after she and Nexus Corp invaded our main facility and refuge. We should be able to lay low there while we analyze the data and formulate a plan."

Parka nodded. "And then what? How do we stop Mizella and Serita? They have the full might of Nexus Corp behind them."

His jaw tightened. "We'll figure that out."

"It won't be easy," she said with doubt.

Zarakano took her hand. The gesture was unexpected, but not unwelcome. "No, it won't be, but we have something they don't."

Parka looked up at him, raising an eyebrow. "What's that?"

He gave her a bolstering smile. "Each other."

Chapter 8 — Zarakano

ZARAKANO APPROACHED the entrance to the old sewage tunnels, his cybernetic eye scanning the area for any potential threats. He turned to Parka, who hung back with a look of disgust on her face.

"Where are you taking me?" she asked, wrinkling her nose at the foul odor emanating from the tunnel entrance.

He kept his voice calm and reassuring. "To a safe house. It's hidden deep underground, accessible only through these old tunnels."

Her eyes widened. "You want us to go in there? It smells awful, and what if it collapses on us?"

"The smell is unpleasant, but the infrastructure is sound," he assured her. "The enclave maintains these routes. They're safer than you might think."

She hesitated, eyeing the dark entrance warily. "I don't know about this. It seems risky."

He placed a hand on her shoulder. "I understand your concern, but we need to move quickly. This is our best option for staying off the grid."

After a moment's consideration, she nodded reluctantly. "All right. I trust you. Lead the way."

He activated the low-light mode in his cybernetic eye and stepped into the tunnel. The musty air filled his nostrils as they descended into the darkness. He heard Parka's footsteps behind him, tentative at first but growing more confident as they progressed.

As they navigated the winding passages, his mind raced with thoughts of Project Hive and the betrayal he'd uncovered. Responsibility pressed down on him, knowing that the fate of countless cyborgs hung in the balance. He also worried for the humans who were simply enhanced and could be controlled with Project Asset.

After what seemed like hours of walking through the damp tunnels, they finally reached a nondescript metal door. He placed his hand on a hidden scanner, and the door slid open with a soft hiss.

Inside, four figures turned to greet them. He recognized his fellow enclave members—Dizzy, a tall, lanky cyborg with enhanced sensory capabilities; Prang, a stocky engineer with reinforced limbs; Kylor, a former combat specialist with advanced targeting systems; and Baz, a quiet but brilliant hacker with a neural interface that rivaled Zarakano's.

"You made it," said Dizzy, relief evident in her voice. "We were starting to worry."

He nodded. "We had a few close calls, but we're here now. This is Parka. She's been instrumental in uncovering Project Hive."

The others murmured greetings as he made his way to the central computer terminal. He sat down and connected himself to the system, feeling the familiar rush of data flowing through his neural pathways. "I've got the data from the old lab. Let's see what we're dealing with."

For the next several hours, the group pored over the information, each focusing on different aspects of Project Hive. His heart sank as the full scope of the plan became clear.

"This is terrible," said Prang, his voice grim. "Serita provided the neural interface technology, and Mizella developed a way to disguise its installation as routine maintenance."

"That's what we've already pieced together," said Parka.

"The data just confirms it," he said, stomach sinking.

Kylor nodded. "They've been building a network of sleeper agents right under our noses."

CYBORG'S LOVE

His cybernetic eye twitched when he dug deeper into the data streaming through his neural nodes. "There's more. The program is set to activate during Unity Day. They're planning to turn hundreds of upgraded cyborgs against the city's leadership."

A heavy silence fell over the room as they processed the information. Baz broke it with a quiet question. "How do we stop this?"

Zarakano settled back in his chair as he considered potential strategies. "We need to warn the city, but we have to be careful. If we move too soon, Mizella and Serita might accelerate their plans and activate the sleeper agents early."

"We don't know who else Nexus Corp has brought into the plan either. We might tip off one of their allies instead of finding help," said Parka before chewing on her lower lip. "We should focus on developing a counter-measure for the neural interface. If we can neutralize their control over the sleeper agents, we might have a chance."

He nodded, impressed by her quick thinking. "Good idea. Prang and Baz, I want you two working on that. Dizzy and Kylor, please start mapping out potential targets and security weaknesses we can exploit. Parka and I will keep sifting through data to see if we can figure out the weak points or find something else useful."

As the others moved to address their tasks, he let the data stream through him, his cybernetic implants seamlessly integrating with the system. Lines of code entered at a dizzying pace, but his enhanced vision processed it all effortlessly.

Parka leaned in close, gaze darting back and forth as she struggled to keep up. "This is incredible. The way you've integrated my repair protocols with your neural interface expertise is like nothing I've ever seen before."

He allowed himself a small nod of satisfaction. "The combination of our knowledge has proven surprisingly effective. However, the true test lies ahead."

He brought up a three-dimensional schematic of the Nexus Corp building, highlighting the executive levels in pulsing red. "Our virus must be uploaded directly to their main servers. The only access point is here." He tapped a finger on the diagram, zooming in on a heavily fortified section.

She frowned, her brow wrinkling while she studied the layout. "That's the section where Serita and Mizella work, isn't it? The security there will be insane."

"Precisely." His tone was grim. "We'll need to devise a strategy to penetrate their defenses without alerting them to our true purpose."

The room fell silent as they both contemplated the enormity of the task before them. He considered various potential scenarios, calculating odds and assessing risks. His cybernetic enhancements allowed him to process information at an inhuman speed, but even he found the challenge daunting.

She suddenly straightened, looking fired up. "What if we don't try to sneak in? What if we walk right through the front door?"

He turned to her, his expression skeptical. "Explain."

"I have Mizella's biometrics." She tapped her datapad, and a holographic 3D image of a DNA strand appeared before them. "It was on file for lab access, and since you downloaded almost everything..." She tapped again, and the image morphed to be the DNA strand superimposing on a Nexus Corp security badge. "We can walk right in if we can nail the cybersecurity."

"Baz," he called, and the programmer turned toward them. "We need you here." He quickly explained the assignment, sure it was in good hands, before turning back to Parka. "Next, we have to figure out a strategy for when we breach the building."

Parka nodded eagerly. "I just need access to an interface node, and a facility that big should have multiple ones in each room. With Mizella's biometrics, we should be able to bypass their safeguards. Then I can

CYBORG'S LOVE

create some kind of malfunction in their systems. Nothing too major, but enough to keep their techs busy."

"And while they're dealing with that, I can interface with their servers to mentally upload the virus."

She frowned. "What if the virus affects you?"

He hesitated. "I'm implanting code. I don't think…"

"We can configure it so the last components don't combine until they recognize a piece of tech or a line of code in the Nexus Corp database," she said.

"Like Mizella's signature code," said Parka with a grin. "Her arrogant insistence on always leaving her mark will be used to our advantage."

He smiled. "Precisely."

They spent the next several hours refining their plan, anticipating potential obstacles and devising contingencies. As the first rays of dawn began to filter through the grimy windows of their hideout, he looked at Parka, her face etched with determination as she made final adjustments to their virus. For a brief moment, he allowed himself to imagine a future where they succeeded—where the sleeper agents were freed, and the city was no longer under the thumb of Nexus Corp's machinations.

"We should rest," he said, breaking the silence. "Tomorrow, we make our move."

Parka nodded, stifling a yawn. As she stood, she placed a hand on his arm. The warmth of her touch sent a jolt through his system.

"We can do this," she said softly.

He was lost for words and simply nodded, watching as she took a step closer, licking her lips. She seemed nervous, but so was he. He'd been with Serita before, thinking he loved her and would marry her, but otherwise, his relationships were lacking—whether with a cyborg or a human. "I…"

She paused. "Do you not want to...?" Her face flushed, and she took a step back. "Sorry. I misread—"

He pulled her closer. "You didn't misread anything. I'm just not that experienced with these matters."

She smiled, looking shy. "Me neither."

With that, he kissed her, and everything else melted away. All that mattered was the feel of her lips on his, the taste of her tongue, and the heat of her body pressed against his. They stumbled across the hallway, and he nudged it open with his foot. A quick glance confirmed it was unclaimed, so he guided her inside. Zarakano kicked the door closed again.

He focused on deepening the kiss now that they had privacy. He wanted to explore every inch of her mouth, to memorize the taste and texture of her lips. He moved his hands over her body, appreciating her humanity contrasted against his cybernetic enhancements. Other than his cybernetic eye, there was no visible clue he was a cyborg, but his synthetic skin wasn't as soft as hers. He appreciated how responsive she was to his touch, arching into him and letting out little moans of pleasure.

His cock hardened, pressing against his pants. He hadn't expected to get aroused so quickly, but he couldn't help himself. She was intoxicating, and he wanted more.

He broke the kiss long enough to unzip the coverall she still wore from earlier. He pushed it off her shoulders, exposing her underlayer. He ran his fingers over the thin material, feeling her nipples harden beneath his touch. He cupped her breasts, squeezing gently, and she gasped.

"Is this okay?" he asked, wanting to be sure she was enjoying herself.

"Yes." Her voice was breathless and eager. "Please don't stop."

He grinned, kissing her again as he continued exploring her body. Slipping his hand lower, he stroked her pussy through the thin underlayer. It was too efficient at wicking away moisture, so he spent a moment removing the rest of the coveralls and helping her shimmy out of the slick underlayer of fabric. Then she was naked before him, and he reached for her again.

She surprised him by pulling away and shaking her head. "Uh uh. You need to get undressed too."

He laughed and started slipping off the black suit that he'd worn under the guise of being a corporate engineer, until he was in his underlayer as well. She stepped forward, running her hands over his chest.

"Wow," she breathed. "You're so muscular."

He shrugged. "Cybernetics require a lot of strength."

She looked up at him, her eyes wide. "Can I see?"

He hesitated, then nodded. He removed the last of his clothing, revealing his fully augmented body. His cock sprang free, already erect and ready for action.

She arched a brow before touching his ocular implant. "Is this really the only indicator of your status?"

He nodded. "Unless you peel away the flesh."

She shook her head. "I'm interested in the flesh…" She gripped his cock. "Not peeling it away though."

He let out a startled laugh. "I'm relieved to hear that, Parka."

She grinned, stroking his shaft. "Now, what am I going to do with this?"

He groaned, thrusting into her grip. "Whatever you want."

Her grin widened, and she dropped to her knees to lick the tip of his cock. He shuddered, gripping her hair as she took him deeper into her mouth. She sucked eagerly, swirling her tongue around his shaft.

He moaned, struggling to keep control. She felt amazing, and he didn't want to come too soon, but she was making it difficult to hold back.

She pulled away, looking up at him with a mischievous glint in her eyes. "Is the pleasure for a cyborg enhanced too?"

He hesitated. "I can't say for sure. I was only twelve when my father brought me to the enclave for enhancement. I've only known sexual pleasure as a cyborg, but you please me well."

She smiled, rising to her feet. "Good. Because I intend to make you come very hard."

He swallowed, nodding. "I look forward to it."

She led him to the bed, pushing him onto his back. He went willingly, watching as she straddled him. She positioned herself above his cock, teasing him with her wet pussy. He groaned, forcing himself to remain still. He gripped her hips, making her cry out in surprise when he lifted her and brought her dripping pussy to his mouth instead of his cock.

She looked unsettled. "What are you doing?"

He frowned up at her. "Pleasuring you. Has no one...?"

Flushing, she shook her head. "I've only had two lovers. With both, I teased them to hardness with my mouth, and then we copulated."

He scowled. "Far too clinical—and inept of your lovers."

She flushed even harder. "It was satisfactory."

He snorted. "Then they weren't satisfying you properly."

She bit her lip, looking uncertain. "And you will?"

"I'll try." He lowered her pussy to his mouth, licking her folds. She tasted delicious, and he lapped at her juices eagerly. She cried out, clutching his head as he explored her with his tongue. He'd be willing to bet she'd never had a true orgasm before, and he intended to be the first—only—to give her that.

He licked and sucked her clit, bringing her closer to the edge. She writhed on top of him, moaning and gasping. When he pushed his tongue inside her, she shuddered and cried out. He felt her inner muscles spasm around his tongue when she climaxed. He kept licking and sucking her, drawing out her pleasure. She screamed, bucking wildly on top of him. He held her firmly in place, continuing to feast on her sweet nectar.

CYBORG'S LOVE

When she finally stopped trembling, he released her. She collapsed beside him, panting heavily. He watched her, waiting for her to recover. After a few minutes, she opened her eyes and looked at him.

"That was incredible," she said softly.

He smiled. "I'm glad you enjoyed it."

She sat up. "I had no idea it was supposed to feel more than nice after the pain stopped."

He scowled again, wishing to find the two men who'd been such selfish jerks. "There should be no pain either after the first time."

She looked skeptical but didn't argue when she glided down his body, gripping his cock to guide it into her pussy. He gasped when she sank down on him, taking him all the way to the hilt. She felt amazing, hot and tight around him. He struggled to stay still, letting her adjust to his size. "Is there pain, Parka?"

She shook her head. "No. Just fullness." She seemed stunned by the sensation.

He waited until she started moving before thrusting upward. They found a rhythm together, moving as one. He gripped her hips, helping her ride him. She threw back her head while bouncing on top of him, crying out in ecstasy. Her breasts swayed enticingly, and he reached up to cup them. She moaned, arching into his touch.

They moved faster, chasing their release. As he stared at her, he instinctively interfaced with her neural implants. The pleasure between them morphed into a mingled, shared experience. He couldn't completely tell what she felt versus what he was feeling. It was amazing. He hadn't achieved this level of interface with anyone. His upgrades to this level hadn't been prepared before Serita's abandonment and betrayal, so he hadn't even experienced it with his former fiancée.

Parka's eyes widened, and she gasped. "Kano? What's happening?"

"We're sharing our pleasure through the neural link."

She shivered, grinding against him. "It feels intense."

He nodded, unable to speak as he focused on maintaining the connection. He wanted to share everything with her, including his emotions. She needed to know how much he cared about her. How special she was to him. How easy it would be to fall in love with her.

As soon as the thought crossed his mind, he realized it was already too late. He was falling in love with her and judging by the intensity of her feelings flowing through the link, she was falling in love with him too. He groaned, surging more deeply inside her as he let go of her hips to grip her hands.

Their gazes locked as they continued moving together. The pleasure built higher and higher until it exploded between them. They cried out simultaneously, clinging to each other as they rode out the waves of ecstasy. She collapsed on top of him, burying her face in his neck. He wrapped his arms around her, holding her close.

After several long moments, she lifted her head to look at him. "I never knew it could be like that."

He smiled, stroking her hair. "Neither did I."

She rested her chin on his chest, gazing at him thoughtfully. "Do you think we can do it again? How long? You must have amazing stamina, being a cyborg." She laughed in a throaty chuckle.

He grinned. "I've got plenty of stamina, but I need some time to recharge." He kissed her gently. "But yes, we can definitely do it again."

She snuggled against him, sighing contentedly. "Good. I want to keep doing it forever."

He chuckled, pulling her closer. "Me too."

They lay together quietly for a while, enjoying the closeness. They should get some sleep, since they had to breach Nexus Corp HQ tomorrow, but she was far too tempting for him to fall asleep just yet. As his cock stirred to life once more, she was clearly ready, already starting to thrust against him since they hadn't completely separated before.

CYBORG'S LOVE

He rolled her onto her back, kissing her passionately. She returned his kisses eagerly while wrapping her legs around his waist. He fully entered her slowly, savoring every inch of her slick heat. She moaned, arching beneath him. He began to move, thrusting deeper and harder as he claimed her. She clung to him, matching his rhythm perfectly. Their bodies moved together in perfect sync, as if they were made for each other.

The pleasure built quickly, and they climaxed together, crying out in unison. He collapsed on top of her, spent and sated. She held him close, stroking his back. "That was incredible," she whispered.

He nodded, nuzzling her neck. "You're amazing."

She giggled softly. "So are you."

"Get some sleep now, Parka. Tomorrow is a busy day." Busy and daunting. What if he lost her? He couldn't think like that, or he'd try to lock her up here in the safe house to keep her protected. She would never agree to that, so he had to focus on completing the mission, not getting paralyzed by what could go wrong. He just couldn't stand to lose her after finding her.

Chapter 9—Parka

PARKA'S PALMS WERE sweaty as she strode into Nexus Corp headquarters, her borrowed executive attire feeling foreign against her skin. The pristine lobby stretched before her and was a jarring contrast to the grime of the Lower District.

She fought to keep her expression impassive, mimicking Mizella's haughty demeanor while she approached the security checkpoint. Prang had fastened an emitter on her blazer to make the world see Mizella, so all she had to do was scrunch her features to seem arrogant and demanding, and the guard would see the familiar Ms. Chong.

The guard's eyes widened as he swiped her forged credentials. "Director Chong, I thought you already checked in today."

Parka waved her hand dismissively. "I went home for a while, but I'm back and I need immediate access to my lab." She hoped they didn't run into the real Mizella while deploying the virus.

She gestured to Zarakano, who stood stoically behind her. "My personal guard will accompany me."

The guard frowned as he swiped Zarakano's badge. "I'm sorry, ma'am, but his credentials aren't clearing. I can't allow him up without proper authorization."

Parka's stomach clenched, but she maintained her cool facade. "Unacceptable. There have been credible threats against me. I refuse to move about unprotected."

The guard shifted uncomfortably. "I understand, Director, but protocols—"

"Override them," she snapped, channeling Mizella's imperious tone. "I'll take full responsibility. I'll have him return to you in ten minutes to sort out this clerical error."

The guard hesitated but nodded reluctantly. "Very well, Director, but please ensure he returns promptly."

She didn't bother to answer, knowing Mizella wouldn't in such circumstances, and strode toward the elevators with Zarakano close behind. As the doors closed, she released a shaky breath. "I thought your badge would pass muster. I almost fainted when it didn't," she said with a weak smile.

His cybernetic eye whirred softly. "Agreed. We need to move quickly."

They exited on a floor below the executive suites, hurrying down a deserted corridor. Her fingers twitched, itching to interface with the building's systems. They rounded a corner and spotted their target—an unattended security node.

After plugging in a bypass drive that she'd made herself, since they were technically illegal without corporate or government authorization—which she lacked—her hands trembled as she tapped on the interface, bypassing firewalls with practiced ease. "I'm in. Creating a distraction now."

She initiated a cascade of minor malfunctions throughout the building—flickering lights and temporary outages in non-critical systems. Nothing catastrophic, but enough to keep the tech teams scrambling and the diagnostic programs focused mainly on identifying the problem, which might give Zarakano easier access to finesse his way in to upload the virus.

His organic eye was closed but visibly moving under his eyelid as he interfaced with the Nexus Corp servers. His cybernetic eye whirred softly, emitting a faint blue glow from the ports along his temples. The virus components uploaded swiftly, and she allowed herself a moment of cautious optimism.

"It's done," he said softly, opening his eyelid. "The virus should activate once it detects Mizella's signature code."

She nodded. "We need to move. Security protocols will—"

The words died in her throat as the door to the server room slid open with a pneumatic hiss. Two corporate enforcers stood in the entrance, their augmented frames filling the doorway. Behind them, Parka caught a glimpse of familiar faces that made her shudder.

Mizella's voice dripped with false sweetness. "How unexpected to discover I entered through security while also in my lab. I always believed it was impossible to be two places at once, so imagine my surprise when front desk security sent someone to retrieve my personal guard."

The guards moved with inhuman speed, seizing them before they could react. Parka struggled against the iron grip, searching for a way out of this mess. It was reassuring that even if they didn't escape, the virus had been uploaded.

"Take them to Conference Room I...for interrogation," said Mizella with a cold smile before turning and exiting.

The enforcers held them tighter, frog marching them from the room. When she tried to go limp, the enforcer started dragging her instead. A glance behind her revealed Zarakano in a similar situation. They were dragged unceremoniously down pristine corridors, and the enforcers barely seemed to notice her continued resistance.

The conference room they were thrust into was sleek and minimalist, dominated by a long obsidian table. Mizella perched on its edge, her perfectly manicured nails tapping an impatient rhythm. Beside her stood a statuesque woman with long brown hair and piercing eyes—Serita Vale. Parka recognized her from Zarakano's memories.

"Zarakano," said Serita tenderly, her lips curving into a smile that didn't reach her eyes. "It's been far too long."

Myriad emotions flashed across Zarakano's face—pain, anger, and betrayal. They vanished as quickly as they appeared, replaced by a mask of cold indifference. "Serita." His voice was devoid of emotion. "I see you've embraced your true nature."

The other woman's smile widened, revealing too-perfect teeth. "Oh, I have, and it's glorious." She took a step forward, her movements unnaturally fluid. "You could have joined us, you know. We could have revolutionized the world together."

"By stripping away free will?" He shook his head. "By turning people into puppets?"

"By perfecting humanity," countered his ex-fiancée. Her eyes gleamed with an almost manic light. "You always were too caught up in your ideals to see the bigger picture."

Without warning, she lunged forward, lashing out. Her fingers morphed into wickedly sharp blades. Zarakano barely managed to dodge the brunt as one of the claws grazed his cheek, drawing a thin line of blood.

Mizella's cold laugh drowned out Parka's cry of alarm. "Oh, this should be entertaining," she said with a chuckle, settling back to watch the spectacle.

The fight that ensued was like nothing Parka had ever witnessed. Serita and Zarakano moved with inhuman speed and precision, their augmented bodies pushing the limits of what should have been possible. Every attack Serita launched, he seemed to anticipate. Every vulnerability she targeted, he had already reinforced.

"I know all your weaknesses," taunted Serita as she aimed a vicious kick at his midsection. "I helped design half your systems, remember?"

He caught her leg, using her momentum to throw her off balance. "And I've spent years patching every backdoor you left."

The fight raged on, neither combatant able to gain a clear advantage. Parka watched in horror and awe, her mind struggling to process the brutal dance before her. She could see the history between them in every move and every counter-attack. This was more than just a physical battle—it was the culmination of years of betrayal and conflicting ideologies.

Suddenly, Serita's eyes flashed with triumph. "Let's see if you've patched this." Her hand flew to a device at her temple, and he stiffened.

Panic flitted through Parka when she recognized the telltale signs of neural interface activation. Serita was trying to disable Zarakano using their old sync frequency.

For a moment, his movements slowed while his systems clearly fought against the intrusion. Then, to her visible shock, he straightened, smirking at his opponent. "Sorry," he said with a grin that showed no regret. "I've picked up a few new tricks in hiding."

With that, he launched into a flurry of attacks that drove Serita back. She snarled in frustration, her perfectly composed veneer cracking.

"Why?" He demanded as they grappled. "Why did you betray everything we stood for?"

Parker leaned forward slightly, wanting to hear the answer for herself. With the possibility of a future between her and Zarakano, she had to make sure all his feelings for Serita were in the past.

Serita's eyes blazed with anger and something that might have been regret. "Because controlling the technology was more important than your enclave's foolish dreams," she shouted. "While you fought to protect some nebulous idea of free will, I saw the potential to perfect it."

Their battle paused for a moment, both combatants breathing heavily. Her next words were quieter, almost wistful. "We could have shaped the future, Kano. We could have guided humanity to its true potential, but I could tell you were too weak to do that. I had to make a choice, and I don't regret my decision to guide and improve cybernetic and organic life."

"By becoming its puppet masters?" His voice was thick with disgust. "That's not guidance. It's tyranny."

Her expression hardened. "You're as blind now as you were then," she said harshly, "And just as expendable."

Parka's heart thundered as she watched the brutal clash between Zarakano and Serita resume. Their inhuman speed and precision made it difficult to follow every move, but she forced herself to remain vigilant. She needed to act, to find a way to turn the tide in their favor.

While Mizella was distracted by the spectacle before her, Parka inched toward the nearest console. She kept her movements slow and deliberate, careful not to draw attention.

"Enjoying the show?" Mizella's voice startled her, dripping with false sweetness. "It's quite something, isn't it? Two advanced creations, tearing each other apart."

She froze, hand inches from the interface, and turned to face Mizella, forcing a neutral expression. "Why are you doing this? What do you hope to gain?"

Her perfect lips curved into a predatory smile. "Absolute control over the future of cybernetic enhancement. No more freelance mechanics mucking about with delicate systems. No more rogue elements threatening the stability we've worked so hard to achieve."

As Mizella spoke, she found the interface with her fingers and initiated a connection, careful to keep her expression calm while she began working behind her back. "You really think you can control an entire population?" she asked, buying time as she tried navigating the system, which proved futile without being able to see the interface. "People will always find ways to resist."

Her former friend laughed, and the sound was sharp and cruel. "Oh, Parka. So naïve. When we're done, there won't be any resistance left to worry about. Our neural interface combined with the advanced AI will ensure complete compliance."

CYBORG'S LOVE

Parka's stomach churned at the thought, but she pressed on. "And what about the right to choose our own path?"

"An illusion." Her old partner sneered. "One that's caused nothing but chaos and suffering. We're offering a better way. A perfect harmony between human and machine. Even the fully organic humans living in the past and refusing to embrace technology can offer something to support the cause. Once their neural interfaces are installed, they'll be part of the network too."

As she continued her villainous monologue, Parka's stomach rolled. Had Mizella ever been the friend and woman she'd thought, or had it all been an illusion? She dared a quick glance behind her, long enough to identify the security icon. She pressed it and initiated a lock-down.

Suddenly, alarms blared throughout the facility. Mizella's head snapped toward the nearest monitor, her eyes widening in shock. "What have you done?"

Parka allowed herself a small, triumphant smile. "Locked out the guards via a lock-down protocol. It's just us now. No more hiding behind your corporate thugs."

Her face contorted with rage. She lunged at Parka, her movements unnaturally fast to indicate she was far more enhanced than she'd been in the past, but Parka was ready. She ducked under Mizella's grasp, using the momentum to slam her palm against another interface node.

A pulse of energy surged through the room, momentarily disrupting Mizella's cybernetic enhancements. She staggered, off-balance for a crucial second. Parka seized the opportunity, delivering a swift kick to Mizella's midsection.

The two women grappled, and her nerves were screaming with fear and adrenaline while she fought to keep Mizella at bay, knowing she was outmatched in terms of raw strength. Parka had something Mizella didn't—an intimate knowledge of cybernetic weak points.

She found the seams where Mizella's enhancements met flesh, applying pressure with her fingers to overload delicate neural connections. Mizella howled in pain and frustration, her movements becoming erratic.

"You can't win," shouted Mizella, her eyes flashing with murderous intent. "You're nothing but a Lower District reject. You don't have the stomach for what needs to be done."

She gritted her teeth, fighting through the pain of Mizella's crushing grip when her adversary seized her arm and started squeezing. "You're right. I don't have the stomach for tyranny and oppression. That's why I'll always fight against people like you."

With a final burst of strength, she slammed Mizella against the central console. She hoped she'd bought enough time for the virus to activate, and she hung back warily as the other woman slumped against the console for a long instant. Was she recovering, strategizing, or being invaded by the virus?

For a moment, nothing happened. Then Mizella's eyes flashed blue before going silver. Her expression went blank as she collapsed against the console. The once-formidable corporate executive now lay motionless, as though awaiting input.

Parka wasted no time. She grabbed Mizella's access badge and limp right hand, using her biometrics to gain full control of the facility's security systems. Alarms blared anew as she turned the full force of Nexus Corp's defenses against Serita while canceling the lock-down currently keeping the guards out. They should come in and target Serita when they did, but she was still nervous.

"Kano," Parka called out, her voice hoarse. "It's done. We need to go."

He rushed toward her, and they were slipping out the second conference room door when corporate enforcers poured in, at least a dozen, and surrounded Serita. If they noticed Parka or Zarakano, they gave no indication of it.

As the virus spread through Nexus Corp's networks, freeing sleeper agents across the city, she and Zarakano made their escape. He kept her

CYBORG'S LOVE

apprised of progress since he was still connected to the database for a time until the encroachment of the virus forced him to disconnect.

They slipped through chaotic corridors, encountering corporate enforcers now focused solely on subduing Serita or suddenly freezing as the virus invaded them. In a matter of minutes, they would be free of the Nexus Corp AI and neural interface, but there was no telling what they might do once they were released from the control of the program. Corporate enforcers already had a certain moral flexibility, and they might try to restrain the two of them once they were no longer acting under the blanket orders Parka had issued.

Once outside, they paused to catch their breath. Parka's legs shook from exertion and adrenaline. She looked at him, seeing the same exhaustion and triumph in his eyes. "We did it," she said, panting through the words.

He nodded, his cybernetic eye whirring as he evaluated their surroundings. "It's not over yet. We need to get to a safe location before notifying the authorities."

She nodded and found another burst of energy to keep going. Every step away from Nexus Corp was liberating, and despite her fatigue, she'd never been more energized due to their victory.

Chapter 10—Zarakano

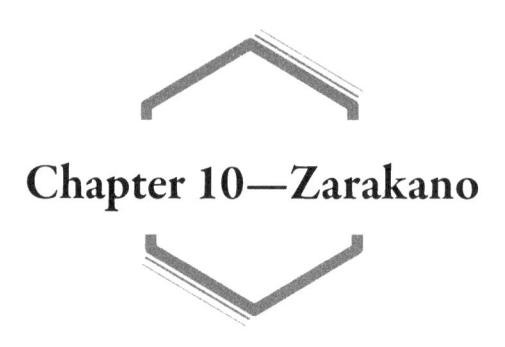

ZARAKANO STOOD IN THE dimly lit laboratory, his cybernetic eye scanning the room filled with recovering cyborgs. The hum of machinery and the occasional beep of diagnostic equipment filled the air. A week had passed since they had thwarted Serita and Mizella's plan, but the work was far from over.

Parka was nearby, hunched over a workbench, moving her fingers deftly as she repaired a cyborg's neural interface. Her short black hair fell across her forehead, and she absently brushed it away, leaving a smudge of grease on her skin. He was captivated by her focus and determination as much as by her beauty.

"How's it going?" he asked, approaching her workstation.

She looked up at him. "Slow but steady. This one's pretty complex. Mizella really did a number on these neural pathways."

He nodded, leaning in to examine her work. The intricacy of the circuitry was impressive, even to his enhanced vision. "You're making good progress. Your expertise with those old clinic protocols is invaluable."

A ghost of a smile crossed Parka's face. "Never thought I'd be using them again, especially not like this."

As they worked side by side, he marveled at how seamlessly they complemented each other. His advanced knowledge of cyborg systems merged perfectly with Parka's innovative repair techniques. Together, they were able to tackle even the most challenging cases.

A commotion near the lab entrance drew their attention. Two former enforcers half-carried, half-dragged an unconscious cyborg into the room. The right side of the cyborg's face was a mess of exposed wiring and damaged synthetic skin.

"What happened?" he asked, moving swiftly to assist them.

One of the enforcers, a burly man with a cybernetic arm, explained, "Found him in the Lower District. Looks like he tried to remove his own implants when they started malfunctioning."

Parka was already clearing a space on a nearby examination table. "Bring him here," she said, her voice calm but urgent.

As they laid down the injured cyborg, his sensors began analyzing the extent of the damage before Parka had even plugged him in for diagnostics. "Multiple system failures. Neural pathways are degrading rapidly."

Parka's hands flew over the cyborg's exposed circuitry, connecting diagnostic tools and beginning emergency repairs. "This is bad, Zarakano. I've never seen corruption like this before."

Zarakano joined her, his own hands moving with inhuman precision as he assisted In the race to stop the degradation. "It's a failsafe Mizella must have implemented. If the cyborg attempts to remove the implants, it triggers a cascade failure."

They worked in tense silence for several minutes, fighting to stabilize the cyborg's systems. He relied heavily on Parka's expertise with jury-rigged repairs, while she in turn depended on his advanced understanding of cyborg physiology.

"I need more power to the neural stabilizer," she said, sounding strained.

Without hesitation, he detached a power coupling from his own arm and connected it to the device. "Use my systems. I can regulate the flow better than the lab's equipment."

Her eyes widened momentarily, but she nodded and made the necessary adjustments. The stabilizer hummed to life, and the erratic beeping of the monitoring equipment began to slow.

"It's working," she said with relief.

Hours passed, and finally, the cyborg's systems stabilized. Parka stepped back, wiping sweat from her forehead with the back of her hand. "We did it," she said, exhaustion and triumph mingling in her voice.

He nodded, disconnecting himself from the equipment. "Yes, we did. Your skills are remarkable."

She looked up at him, a genuine smile spreading across her face. "We make a good team, don't we?"

Zarakano knew just how true her words were. Their combined knowledge and skills had achieved something he wasn't sure either of them could have done alone. More than that, he had a sense of trust and connection with Parka that he hadn't experienced with anyone, even his comrades in the enclave, and certainly not with Serita. He'd never loved her—just the version of whom she'd pretended to be.

"We do," he said softly. "I've never worked with anyone quite like you before."

Her cheeks reddened slightly at the compliment. "I've certainly never worked with anyone like you either. A cyborg from a secret enclave with more knowledge about neural interfaces than I've ever seen? You're pretty unique."

As they began cleaning up the workspace, he reflected on their partnership. He had always prided himself on his self-sufficiency, but working with Parka had shown him the strength that could come from true collaboration.

"Parka," he said, his voice uncharacteristically hesitant. "I want you to know I... appreciate what we've accomplished here. Not just with this patient, but with all of it. Taking down Mizella, helping these cyborgs—I couldn't have done it without you."

Parka paused in her work, looking up at him with surprise. "That's... Thank you, Kano. I feel the same way. When Mizella betrayed me, I thought I'd never be able to trust anyone again, but working with you is amazing. I feel like we're really making a difference."

He nodded as warmth filled his chest. "We are, and I believe we can do even more. The authorities may be ignoring what's happening, but we can continue to help these cyborgs, to undo the damage Mizella has done."

"You want to keep working together?" she asked with a hint of hopefulness in her voice.

"Yes," he said without hesitation. "Our combined knowledge and skills are formidable. We can accomplish things neither of us could do alone."

Parka smiled, extending her hand to him. "Partners, then?"

Zarakano took her hand. "Partners."

LATER THAT NIGHT, HE sat at the small table in the apartment above the secret lab, watching Parka stab at her synthicated dinner with more force than necessary. The harsh overhead light cast shadows across her face, accentuating the lines of frustration etched there.

"I can't believe the authorities haven't done anything," she said with anger. "It's like Mizella and Serita never existed."

He nodded, his cybernetic eye whirring softly as he analyzed her expression. "The city officials are hesitant to challenge Nexus Corp. Their influence runs deep."

Parka snorted. "That's an understatement. They've got their tentacles in everything."

He set down his fork, the metallic clink echoing in the small space. "I may have a way to find out more."

Her eyes widened. "How?"

CYBORG'S LOVE

"I can infiltrate their security systems. I left a backdoor during my last access to deploy the virus."

Parka leaned forward, her food obviously forgotten. "Is that safe though? What if they detect you?"

"The risk is minimal. If they haven't detected the backdoor by now and shut it down, it's unlikely they will."

She chewed her lip, clearly considering. "Okay. Do it."

He closed his eyes, his cybernetic implants humming to life. For several minutes, he sat motionless while his consciousness navigated the complex digital landscape of Nexus Corp's security network.

When he opened his eyelids, she was staring at him intently. "Well?"

"They've taken action," he said. "Serita and Mizella are in custody, along with several other high-ranking officials involved in the plan."

Parka's eyebrows shot up. "Really? Why hasn't this been made public?"

"They're keeping it quiet to avoid panic, but probably also to cash in on what Serita and Mizella had developed. The scale of the conspiracy was extensive."

"What about Mizella?" she asked, her voice tight. "Is she...okay?" She shuddered, probably recalling how blank the other woman had been.

He hesitated, knowing the complex history between Parka and her former friend. "The virus we uploaded seems to have had an unexpected effect on her neural implants. Maybe it hit her so hard because her signature code caused the elements to combine, and she was the first cybernetic organism to get the full virus. She's been wiped clean. There's no trace of her original personality or memories."

Her face paled. "She's gone? Completely?"

He nodded. "She can't hurt anyone again, Parka, but she's also not the person you once knew."

Parka pushed away from the table, pacing the small room. "I don't know how to feel about that. I hated what she'd become, but she wasn't always like that." She sighed. "Or maybe she was, and I never really knew her at all."

He watched her, understanding the conflict in her emotions. "It's okay to mourn who she was, even if you don't regret stopping what she became."

She stopped pacing, turning to face him. "What happens now? To us and to your enclave?"

Zarakano stood to scrape his leftovers into the recycler. "We return to obscurity. Continue our work outside the rules of Nexus Prime, improving lives where we can."

"Just like that?" she asked. "After everything we've done?"

"It's what we do best." He shrugged "Operating in the shadows, making a difference without drawing attention, and without needing permission from a city held hostage to corporate interests."

Parka stepped closer to him, searching his face. "And where do I fit into all of this?"

He cupped her cheek. "With me, if you want, and the rest of the enclave agrees. Your skills and enthusiasm would be invaluable to our cause." He lowered his voice. "Your passion is also intoxicating, and I want to see more of it."

She leaned into his touch with a smile. "I'd like that." She moved to sit on the sofa in the corner of the room. "I want to know everything if I'm going to be part of it."

Zarakano joined her, his larger frame dwarfing the piece of furniture. "It started decades ago, when a group of cyborg scientists and engineers realized the potential dangers of unchecked cybernetic advancement in the wrong hands. We've always operated on the fringes. Developing technology to help rather than control, to enhance life rather than replace it."

CYBORG'S LOVE

"That sounds incredible," she said, "But how do you stay hidden? Surely, Nexus Corp and others have tried to find you?"

He nodded. "They have, and they succeeded with Serita's undercover operation, but in general, our security measures are extensive. We use a combination of advanced cloaking technology and misdirection. Most of our work is done through intermediaries, who don't even know they're working for us."

Parka's eyes widened. "Like me when you first approached me after the enforcer entered my shop. You didn't tell me who you really were."

He nodded, wincing. "It was necessary at the time."

She nodded too. "I understand why, and now I'll be part of all that?"

"If you choose to be. It won't be easy. We'll be constantly moving and always watching our backs, but the work we do makes a difference."

Parka reached out, taking his hand in hers. The contrast between her soft skin and his metallic fingers was stark, but somehow, it felt right. "I'm in," she said firmly. "Whatever it takes."

Warmth spread through his chest, a sensation his cybernetic systems couldn't quite categorize. "Thank you, Parka. Your trust means more than I can express."

◈

A FEW WEEKS LATER, Zarakano stood at the console in a safe house, having moved back there once they'd had no more need for the secret clinic. They hadn't gone back to a more central enclave location though, because not enough members had voted to approve an outsider joining. He wouldn't leave Parka, so there they were. He hoped his stubbornness would overcome the others' resistance to change.

His cybernetic eye whirred as it processed the incoming data. The room hummed with the soft glow of holographic displays and the muted beeps of monitoring equipment. He frowned as he read the reports from their underground operatives across different cities.

"Parka," he called out with some urgency. "You need to see this."

She looked up from her workstation, where she had been tinkering with a neural interface prototype. She set down her tools and walked over to him. "What is it?" she asked, looking at the holographic display.

He gestured to the scrolling text. "Reports from our operatives in other cities. It seems Nexus Corp's influence extends far beyond Nexus Prime. They've been manipulating cybernetic systems on a global scale."

Her eyes widened as she read the details. "This is extensive. Neural suppression in Andorova, forced upgrades in Nexus North, and backdoor access to government cyborgs in Shoyonai..."

He nodded grimly. "Serita's arrest may have dealt a blow to their operations here, but the threat is far from over."

She ran a hand through her short black hair, leaving it slightly disheveled. "I should have known Mizella's ambitions wouldn't be limited to just one city. She always thought big, so she probably planned to go even beyond the planet."

He turned to face her, his expression softening slightly. "You couldn't have known the full extent of their plans. What matters now is how we respond."

Parka nodded. "So, what's our next move? We can't exactly hop on a shuttle and start fixing cyborgs all over the world."

"No, but we can expand our network. Share our knowledge with trusted individuals in these cities. Create a web of resistance against corporate control."

Her eyes glistened with excitement. "Like an underground railroad for cyborgs. We could set up secure communication channels, share repair techniques, and maybe even develop some kind of universal anti-tampering software..."

CYBORG'S LOVE

As she spoke, her hands moved animatedly, sketching invisible diagrams in the air. He was captivated by her enthusiasm and her brilliant mind already racing ahead to solutions.

"Exactly," he said, smiling. "It'll take time and resources. We'll need a permanent base of operations, somewhere secure where we can coordinate our efforts with others to support us."

Parka's excitement dimmed. "The enclave? You said the others voted against letting me in. Outsiders aren't allowed..."

He stepped closer to her. "I've found a loophole. If you become my wife, they'll let you in. I want you to come live at the enclave. Work with me there. Live with me and build a future together as my partner in every sense."

She audibly gasped. "You're asking me to leave everything behind?" She frowned then. "That's not much these days..."

"Think of the difference we could make together. We've already proven how effective we are as a team."

She was quiet for a moment, her gaze drifting back to the holographic display with its litany of corporate abuses. When she looked back at him, there was a new resolve in her expression. "I want to, but I don't want to marry you just so we can work together with the enclave's blessing. It has to be because of real feelings between us."

He tilted his head, waiting for her to continue.

Parka took a deep breath. "I'm falling in love with you. I know it's complicated, with you being a cyborg and me being human, and we have this huge mission ahead of us, but I can't pretend it isn't happening, and I won't pretend to be okay with a fake marriage just to get access to the enclave."

His cybernetic systems registered a spike in his heart rate as a rush of endorphins flooding his system. He took Parka's hand. "There's nothing fake about it. I'm falling too. The truth is... I think I've already fallen. Completely."

Her eyes widened as a smile spread across her face. She stepped closer, eliminating the last bit of space between them. "Really? Even with all the complications, and all the differences between us?"

He nodded while cupping her cheek. "Those differences are part of what makes us strong together."

She leaned into his touch, her eyelids fluttering closed for a moment. When she opened them again, her expression became pure joy. "Then let's do this," she said. "Let's change the world, one cyborg at a time, and one night at a time," she said in a huskier tone.

He leaned down to claim her mouth for a deep, passionate kiss. It was a promise, a declaration, and a merging of two worlds. As they stood there in the glow of the holographic displays, the future stretched out before them—uncertain and challenging, but full of possibility.

When they finally broke apart, both slightly breathless, he rested his forehead against hers. "Welcome to the enclave, partner," he said softly.

She grinned up at him. "Partner in all things?"

"In all things," he confirmed, sealing the promise with another kiss. "Wife."

"Not yet, but soon," she said with a small smile.

As they turned back to the console, hands still intertwined, the holographic display continued to scroll with reports from around the world, but now, instead of a daunting challenge, it looked like an opportunity to make a real difference, to protect those who couldn't protect themselves, and to forge a new path forward with the woman he loved at his side.

Zarakano gently squeezed her hand. "Ready to get to work?"

Parka nodded with determination. "With you? Always."

Epilogue—Parka

A YEAR LATER, PARKA tapped the holographic interface, adjusting the quantum resonance frequencies of the cybernetic shielding protocol. The lab hummed with energy from machines and minds working in harmony. Through her neural sync with Zarakano, she sensed his pride and love wash over her, which was like a warm current that buoyed her spirit.

"Zarakano, look at this," she said, gesturing to the display. "I've managed to integrate the old clinic protocols with the enclave's quantum stabilizers. It's creating a feedback loop that actually strengthens the shield instead of destabilizing it."

He moved closer, his cybernetic eye whirring as he examined her work. "Impressive. You've come so far since we first met. Your innovations are pushing us beyond what we thought possible."

She grinned. "It's all thanks to you and the enclave. I never imagined I'd be working with technology this advanced." She turned back to the interface, making a few more adjustments. The holographic display shifted, revealing a complex lattice of energy patterns. "If we can implement this on a larger scale, we might be able to protect entire districts from neural interference."

He nodded, resting his hand on her shoulder. "It could change everything. No more forced upgrades, and no more corporate control over people's minds."

She leaned into his touch, savoring the connection. Even after a year, the comfort of their neural sync still amazed her. It was like always having a piece of Zarakano with her, and a constant reminder of their bond.

"Do you ever miss your old life?" he asked suddenly. "Before all this?"

She paused, considering the question. "Sometimes, I miss the simplicity of it. Just fixing things and not worrying about saving the world." She turned to face him. "But I wouldn't trade this for anything. What we're doing here, and what we've built together, is more than I ever dreamed possible."

He smiled, the expression softening his usually stern features. "I'm glad you're here, wife. I don't know if I could have done any of this without you."

She smiled. "We did this together. Partners, remember, husband?"

They worked late into the night, fine-tuning the shielding protocols and running simulations. As the lab's systems powered down for the evening, a wave of exhaustion washed over her. She stretched, her muscles protesting after hours of focused work.

"Ready to call it a night?" he asked, already shutting down his workstation.

She nodded, stifling a yawn. "Definitely. I think my brain might explode if I look at one more line of code."

They made their way through the enclave's winding corridors, the soft blue glow of bioluminescent panels lighting their path. The refuge was quiet at this hour, most of its inhabitants already retired for the night.

As they entered their quarters, a flutter of nervousness hit her. She'd been waiting for the right moment to share her news, and now, in the privacy of their home, it finally felt right.

Zarakano must have sensed her change in mood through their neural link. He turned to her, his brow gathered with concern. "Is everything all right, Parka? Your neural patterns seem agitated."

CYBORG'S LOVE

She took a deep breath, steadying herself. "There's something I need to tell you." She took his hand, guiding him to sit beside her on their bed. The familiar comfort of their shared space gave her courage.

"What is it?" he asked, his voice gentle.

Parka looked into his eyes, organic and synthetic, yet so full of warmth and love. She squeezed his hand. "I'm pregnant," she whispered.

For a moment, he was perfectly still, his cybernetic systems clearly processing the information. Then his face broke into a wide grin, joy radiating through their neural link. "Pregnant?" he repeated, his voice filled with wonder. "When did you find out?"

Parka laughed, relief and happiness bubbling up inside her. "I've suspected for a few days, but I wanted to be sure before I told you. I ran the tests—four of them—this morning while you were in that strategy meeting."

He pulled her into a tighter embrace, trembling slightly. "A baby," he murmured against her hair. "Our baby."

She melted into his arms, tears of joy pricking at her eyes. "We never really talked about it. With everything going on, it seemed like such a distant possibility, but now..."

He pulled back, cupping her face in his hands. "Now it's real, and it's wonderful."

She placed her hand over her still-flat stomach, marveling at the life growing inside her. "I can't believe we're going to be parents," she said, a hint of nervousness creeping into her voice. "Do you think we're ready?"

His chuckle warmed her heart. "Ready? Probably not, but we'll figure it out, just like we have with everything else." He placed his hand over hers. "This child will have the best of both worlds," he said softly. "Purely human, but he or she can have access to advance cybernetics when they're older..." He grinned. "They'll be perfect whether they remain unaltered, enhanced, or become fully cybernetic."

"I agree." Parka leaned in, pressing her forehead against his. Through their neural link, she could feel his excitement, his love, and a touch of fear that mirrored her own. "We're going to need to make some changes around here," she said, glancing around their quarters. "I don't think a lab is the safest place for a baby."

He nodded. "We'll convert the spare room into a nursery, and we'll need to adjust our work schedules to make sure one of us is always available."

Parka smiled. "You're going to be an amazing father, Kano."

He kissed her then, soft and sweet, while pouring all his love and devotion into the gesture. When they parted, she yawned, the day's excitement catching up with her.

"We should get some rest," he said, gently guiding her to lie down. "You're going to need it."

As they settled into bed, she curled into his side, resting her head on his chest. The steady hum of his cybernetic systems mixed with the sound of his heartbeat to create a soothing lullaby. "Kano?" she murmured, sleep already tugging at the edges of her consciousness.

"Yes, love?"

"I'm scared, but I'm also so, so happy."

His arm tightened around her as he pressed a kiss to the top of her head. "Me too," he whispered.

As she drifted off to sleep, visions of the future filled her mind. A future where their child would grow up in a world free from corporate control and forced upgrades. A future where humans and cyborgs could live in harmony, benefiting from the strengths of both.

It wouldn't be easy. There were still battles to be fought but lying in the arms of the man she loved, with new life growing inside her, Parka was ready.

CYBORG'S LOVE

Get The Whole Series

Welcome to a planet of cyborgs and their human mates. This is a joint venture with me (writing as Aurelia Skye), Juno Wells, and Eden Ember. More titles are coming soon![1]

---

[1]. https://kittunstall.com/series/series-biocircuit-nexus/

About Juno

JUNO WELLS GREW UP on Florida's Space Coast, watching the shuttles take off from Cape Canaveral. When she hit college, her childhood fantasies about space travel turned highly romantic. Now her mind reels with space adventures of fantastic alien lords in distant galaxies, and the earth women they love.

Wells' stories explore the complex, sensual relationships between inhabitants of different star systems. There are always happy endings just as there is always a new world to explore.

Have a comment? Make first contact with Juno at authorjunowells@gmail.com.

Get her newsletter: subscribeto.eo.page/junowells (Get a free book!)

About Aurelia

AURELIA SKYE IS THE pen name Kit Tunstall uses when writing science fiction romance. It's simply a way to separate the myriad types of stories she writes so readers know what to expect with each "author."

USA Today Bestselling author Kit Tunstall lives in the Midwest with her husband and two sons. She enjoys writing several genres and subgenres, but almost everything she writes has a strong romantic element.

Website[1]

---

1. http://www.kittunstall.com

Did you love *Cyborg's Love*? Then you should read *Mated To The Cyborg General*[2] by Aurelia Skye!

Celestial Mates—Romancing the Galaxy... One moment, completely human and modern-day Carrie Morgan is crocheting in her living room. The next second, a peach alien claiming to be a Celestial Mates agent transports her and her dog four hundred years into the future. He leaves her there to be discovered by her supposed fated mate—a blue-skinned cyborg general. The sly agent failed to mention a few things, like the fact humans and cyborgs are at war with each other! She's certain Freydon Rote is crazy, but as she gets to know the cyborg general, she realizes maybe there's something to the claim that DVS84 is meant to be her mate. Passionate nights further convince her that perhaps she's in the right place at the right time to find her happy

---

2. https://books2read.com/u/bwWyNY

3. https://books2read.com/u/bwWyNY

ending—if she survives all the challenges of her new environment. Can a human woman find true love with a cyborg general fighting against her species? Find out in this latest installment in the Celestial Mates (and first in the Cybernetic Hearts) series, brought to you by *USA Today* bestselling author Kit Tunstall, writing as Aurelia Skye.

Also by Aurelia Skye

Alien Baby Pact
Baby For The Brundle Commander
Baby For The Serp General
Alien Baby Pact Compilation
Baby For The Grimlock General
Baby For The Palantir Chief
Baby For The Alphan Captain
Baby For The Mosaic Med Chief
Baby For The Tark Commander

Alien Baby Pakt
Alien Baby Pakt Zusammenstellung

BioCircuit Nexus
Cyborgs' Origins
Cyborg's Tether
Cyborg's Love

Celestial Mates
Wrong Place, Right Mate
Destined For The Drakari Warlords

Cybernetic Hearts
Mated To The Cyborg General
Claimed By The Cyborg Commander
Fated For The Cyborg Officer
Meant For The Cyborg Captain
Baby For The Cyborg General
Cybernetic Hearts: Complete Series
Cœurs Cybernétiques: Série Complète

Dazon Agenda
Written In The Stars
Alien's Babies
Diplomatic Affairs
Moon Madness
Across The Stars
Emperor's Assassin Bride
Dazon Agenda: Complete Collection
Compilation de l'Agenda Dazon

Evershift Haven
Pumpkin Spice and Orc's Delight
Howls & Harvest

Future Fairytales
Hooked

Guerriers Blessés
Chassé
Inlassable
Marqué
Justice
Compilation Guerriers Blessés

Harrow Bay
Hell Gates & Hot Flashes
Nightmares & Night Sweats
Warlocks & Wrinkles
Love Spells & Liver Spots
Phantasms & Presbyopia
Vampires & Varicose Veins
Mermaids & Mood Swings
Séances & Sagging Skin
Necromancy & Knee Pains
Marids & Memory Loss
Devil Deals & Dizzy Spells
Happy Endings & New Beginnings
Harrow Bay, Volume 1
Hellhounds & Mistletoe
Harrow Bay, Volume 2
Harrow Bay, Volume 3
Harrow Bay Complete Series

Harrow Bucht Serie
Höllentore & Hitzewallungen
Alpträume Und Nachtschweiß
Hexenmeister & Falten
Liebeszauber Und Leberflecken
Phantasmen Und Alterssichtigkeit
Vampire und Krampfadern
Meerjungfrauen Und Stimmungsschwankungen
Séancen Und Schlaffe Haut
Nekromantie Und Knieschmerzen
Marids und Gedächtnisverlust
Teufelsgeschäfte Und Schwindelzauber
Happy Ends Und Neuanfängen
Höllenhunde & Mistelzweige

Hell Virus
Catching Hell
Surviving Hell
Bleeding Hell
Raising Hell
Sharing Hell

Howls Romance
The Jaguar Alpha's Forbidden Lover
CEO Wolf Shifter's Surprise Twins

Northstar Shifters
Northstar Heir's Scarred Mate

Olympus Station
Station Commander's Surrogate
Alien Prince's Secret Baby
Security Agent's Alien Bartender
Olympus Station Compilation

SpicyShorts
Music In My Heart
Kilted Tentacle Monster: A Search for True Love

Sweet Escapes
Hook & Wendy

The Haunting of Clara Gray
Ghostly Awakening
Ghostly Harmonies

Three Crones Inn
Vastly Inn-proved
Ghastly Intentions

Grave Inn-tervention
Ghostly Inn-heritance
Three Crones Inn Compilation

True North
True North #1: Death & Deception
True North #2: Rescued & Revelations
True North #3: Fire & Ice
True North #4: Enemies & Lovers
True North #5: Truth & Tiranog
True North #6: Fight & Flight
True North #7: Love & Loss

Wounded Warriors
Relentless
Marked
Justice
Wounded Warriors Collection
Hunted

Standalone
Reluctant Companion
Princess By Mistake
Fire Lord's Assistant
True North
Dragon Laird's Witch
Alien General's Rebel Consort
Tempted By Demons

Enemy Combatant
Grotesquerie
Mistaken Bounty
Wahre Richtung
Power Surges & Amorous Urges
Taken By The Orc General
Compilation Alien Baby Pact

Also by Juno Wells

Alien Baby Pact
Baby For The Brundle Commander
Baby For The Serp General
Alien Baby Pact Compilation
Baby For The Grimlock General
Baby For The Palantir Chief
Baby For The Alphan Captain
Baby For The Mosaic Med Chief
Baby For The Tark Commander

Alien Baby Pakt
Alien Baby Pakt Zusammenstellung

BioCircuit Nexus
Cyborgs' Origins
Cyborg's Tether
Cyborg's Love

Dazon Agenda
Written In The Stars
Alien's Babies
Diplomatic Affairs
Moon Madness
Across The Stars
Emperor's Assassin Bride
Dazon Agenda: Complete Collection
Compilation de l'Agenda Dazon

Galactic Alphas
Alpha's Omega
Buying His Omega
Claiming His Omega
Galactic Alphas Compilation

Standalone
Alien General's Rebel Consort
Compilation Alien Baby Pact

Milton Keynes UK
Ingram Content Group UK Ltd.
UKHW021058031224
452078UK00010B/682